"Want to go for a drive?"

Abby did. Desperately. The intensity scared her. "Aren't you tired of Christmas lights and holiday displays by now?"

"Are you tired of police work?"

"A little," she confessed, startling a laugh out of both of them.

"Take a drive with me. I'll buy you a drink."

"You're a terrible flirt."

"So I've been told." Riley winked, opening the passenger door of his truck for her.

"No, I mean you're really bad at it."

"You want me to up my game?"

Yes. No. Uncertain, she pulled the door shut. When he slid into the driver's seat, she said, "I don't want any games. I want you to be yourself."

"Easy enough." He stared at her for a moment that went on and on, and she realized she was holding her breath. "What you see is what you get, Abby."

THE HUNK NEXT DOOR

USA TODAY Bestselling Authors

DEBRA WEBB &
REGAN BLACK

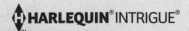

HARLEQUIN® INTRIGUE®

For Mark, my personal hero, who always knows when I need encouraging words, quiet space or dark chocolate.
And many, many thanks to Deb for inviting me into this wonderful new adventure! Regan

To my hero, Nonie! Though four decades have passed since we first met, you continue to be the only hero for me!

Debra

ISBN-13: 978-0-373-69795-3

The Hunk Next Door

Copyright © 2014 by Debra Webb

Recycling programs for this product may not exist in your area.

Printed in U.S.A.

www.Harlequin.com

ABOUT THE AUTHORS

DEBRA WEBB, born in Alabama, wrote her first story at age nine and her first romance at thirteen. It wasn't until she spent three years working for the military behind the Iron Curtain—and a five-year stint with NASA—that she realized her true calling. A collision course between suspense and romance was set. Since then the *USA TODAY* bestselling author has penned more than one hundred novels, including her internationally bestselling Colby Agency series.

REGAN BLACK, a *USA TODAY* bestselling author, writes award-winning, action-packed novels featuring kick-butt heroines and the sexy heroes who fall in love with them. Raised in the Midwest and California, she and her family, along with their adopted greyhound, two arrogant cats and a quirky finch, reside in the South Carolina Lowcountry where the rich blend of legend, romance and history fuels her imagination.

CAST OF CHARACTERS

Abigail Jensen—The beloved and fearless police chief of Belclare, Maryland, busts a drug trafficking ring that's been laundering money for a terrorist cell.

Riley O'Brien—One of Thomas Casey's elite Specialists, he goes undercover to protect Chief Jensen from a pending terrorist retaliation.

Thomas Casey—The director of the Specialists has one last task force to assemble as he nears retirement.

Martin Filmore—As the current president of the Belclare historical society, he is concerned Chief Jensen's new security measures will ruin the annual Christmas Village.

Deke Maynard—An artist bordering on reclusive, Deke moved to Belclare three years ago and has had his eye on Abigail, fostering a friendship with the potential for romance.

Prologue

Washington, D.C.
Friday, November 25, 6:10 p.m.

Thomas Casey, director of the elite team known as the Specialists, leaned back in his chair and watched the footage filling his computer monitor one last time. The woman on the screen stared directly at the camera, her expression one of fearlessness.

"Let this be a clear message to anyone with criminal intent," she announced in a steely tone. "Belclare will not stand for drug activity on our docks or criminal action in our town. We will stand against you and we *will* seize your product, your people and your money at every opportunity. No matter your affiliation or intent, this community will not be used for illicit gain."

The knock on his closed office door was a welcome distraction. Thomas muted the feed. "Come in."

The beautiful face of his wife, Johara di Rossi, peered around the door. "Is it safe to come in?"

He motioned her forward. It was still a thrill to realize they were married, that he had the rest of his life to make up for lost time. No one had ever made him feel that way... no one but Jo.

Her smile wide, she stepped into the office. "If you're sure. Your face tells a different story."

Removing his glasses, he rubbed the bridge of his nose. "Am I running late?" He checked his watch, wishing he had the luxury of forgetting this video in favor of the standing dinner date with his wife. But when the President of the United States issued a directive, department heads were expected to drop everything and act immediately.

"No." She strolled across the room and leaned over his desk to give him a kiss. "I was out this way and thought we could ride to dinner together."

"That's fine. I just have one last meeting to take care of first."

A knock at the door interrupted him. Damn. One of these days very soon he intended to make personal time a priority.

Jo winked at him. "I'll wait for you at reception."

"Thanks." He watched her go, grateful he'd been given a second chance with the one woman who mattered and that she understood the urgency of his work.

Ever the professional, Jo didn't exchange a word with the man in a charcoal-gray suit who walked in as she walked out.

"Close the door," Thomas said to his visitor. "And take a seat."

Specialist Riley O'Brien followed both orders with a quiet "Sir."

Thomas looked from the image of the Belclare police chief on his computer monitor to the man sitting patiently in front of him. "I appreciate your quick response."

"Yes, sir."

Thomas hesitated. One more sign that his decision to retire was the right one. A man in his position couldn't afford to regret the tasks he assigned, but what he needed from O'Brien was extreme even for a Specialist.

He pushed away his own bias, pushed aside the memories of his own career and focused on O'Brien. All of his Specialists excelled in the obvious areas necessary for a successful covert operative, and each of them had a unique set of skills. It was O'Brien's distinctive résumé that made him the perfect fit for this operation.

"O'Brien, you've been selected as the first agent for a new task force. Before you agree, let me assure you, you can turn this assignment down without penalty."

The younger man settled a little deeper into the chair, his eyes intent. "Understood, sir."

Already, they both knew he would agree. Thomas leaned forward, bracing his forearms on his desk. "I'm asking you to take on a deep-cover assignment. We will rework your background accordingly. You'll keep your name, but your new address will be Belclare, Maryland."

"On the Chesapeake Bay?"

"You've heard the latest news out of Belclare." Thomas turned his computer monitor around for O'Brien.

"Kind of hard to miss, sir."

Thomas concurred. "This new team is tasked with embedding agents on long-term assignments where threats are expected."

"And the end date, sir?"

"None." Thomas cleared his throat. "In the short term, you are assigned to keep the Belclare police chief, Abigail Jensen, alive."

"You believe retaliation is imminent?"

"Yes. She's done a hell of a job, but she's made herself a target. They might come after her directly or they may attack another target in town to cause trouble first. It could be next week, or next year, or..."

"A decade down the road," O'Brien finished for him.

"Yes." On a sigh, Thomas leaned back into the supple leather executive chair and studied the agent on the opposite side of his desk. "Based on the intel, I feel confident you'll see some action right away, but this is a lifetime commitment I'm asking for."

"All right." O'Brien shifted forward, propping his elbows on his knees, his gaze on the floor. "Any backup?"

"Not on the ground."

O'Brien lifted his gaze to Thomas's. "Can you be more specific?"

Fair question. "You'll have a way to upload any relative intelligence to our analysts, but I expect you to take action as necessary to protect our nation's interests against terrorism. We can give you anything you need. We just can't be *there* in under an hour."

O'Brien nodded his understanding.

"Belclare is too close to D.C. and other valuable targets," Thomas went on. "We've heard disturbing chatter about a sleeper cell in the area."

"What kind of cause?"

While that wasn't a question he would typically answer, this wasn't a typical assignment. "The drug shipment the chief intercepted was meant to fund a known terrorism splinter group gaining a foothold here in the States. Homeland Security has been monitoring Jensen's email since the speech went viral. Some of the hate mail is too specific for an outsider. Additionally, we've tracked a recent shipment of stolen military detonators to Baltimore."

Throughout his career, Thomas had led by example, never asking more of his agents than he asked of himself. *Until today.* Looking across the desk, he put himself in O'Brien's shoes and wondered how he might have responded if he'd been offered a similar assignment in his early thirties. "Take your time, O'Brien. Think it through."

Normally he wouldn't drop something like this on an agent with limited field experience, but the key to this task force came down to the ability to blend in. To be the guy next door. Raised in an orphanage, O'Brien had been melding with his community and surroundings his whole life. During his two years as a Specialist, he'd worked behind the scenes, offering physical and technical support during various operations. An agent with less field experience meant the tech experts would have less to scrub away and an easier time rebuilding the personal history. Also in his favor for this particular operation, O'Brien had proved to be a natural when it came to managing explosives.

A few more seconds of silence ticked by and then O'Brien nodded, his gaze resolute. "Count me in, sir."

"Good." Especially for the police chief and her town, Thomas mused. "Belclare will be finishing preparations for their annual Christmas Village when you arrive. With your experience in construction, you'll be able to find work easily."

"But you want me to stay on in the area after that's over."

"Yes. You'll need to make yourself at home within the community. Chief Jensen will need you, whether she knows it or not. We'll get the necessary background ready."

"Thank you, sir."

Thomas stood and reached across the desk to shake the agent's hand. "Let me be the first, and quite possibly the only person, to thank you for your service."

Chapter One

Belclare Police Station
Wednesday, November 30, 9:50 a.m.

Riley measured the span of the double doorway and clipped the tape measure back on his tool belt. He'd picked up work with the company in charge of transforming Belclare into a Christmas extravaganza just as the director suggested. Riley considered his assignment off to a stellar start when he was sent over to decorate the police station.

"She's in a meeting." The young cop working the reception desk behind him was having trouble with one of Belclare's citizens. "May I take a message?"

"She's a young hothead is what she is," the irritated older man replied. "The historical society has never been handcuffed in this manner. I will not stand for it. The tourists expect..."

Riley continued tacking holiday garland around the door frame as the man droned on about tourism, children and intrusive patrols.

"Safety is our utmost priority," the young officer said. "From our chief right down to our newest recruits."

Preach on, kid, Riley thought. Belclare would need every patrol if only half of the chatter about retaliation was true. Chief Jensen was in serious trouble. Via email, the director had kept him in the loop with the most direct threats to help Riley identify the locals who no doubt had to be involved. At the moment, this guy from the historical society was quickly gaining himself a spot at the top of the list.

Riley stepped down the ladder to gather up the next length of evergreen woven with velvet ribbon and colorful ornaments. This town pulled out all the stops for the holiday. He couldn't see why the police station needed decorating, but the work put him close to the chief. At this stage, she didn't have a clue that by doing an excellent job as chief, she'd not only protected her town, she'd also put them in more jeopardy.

Though he hadn't yet seen more than a photo of the lady with the tough-as-nails reputation, Riley admired her efficiency.

The older man with the beef against the chief's new security requirements was turning red in the face as he continued his protest.

Finished with the doorway, Riley decided a break in the tension was needed. "I'm taking a break for hot chocolate," he said to no one particular. "Can I get anyone anything?"

The old man swiveled around, scowling at him. "Who are you?" He turned back to the young cop behind the desk. "Do you know *him?* He might very well be an assassin right here in our midst. Now who isn't being careful enough?"

"Don't worry about me," Riley said, laughing off the accusation. "I just follow the work. Riley O'Brien." He stuck out his hand, but the older man refused to take it.

"Martin Filmore, president of the Belclare Historical Society," he replied, a sour look on his weathered face.

"Pleased to meet you." Riley gave him a big smile and hooked his thumbs into his tool belt. "Can I get you anything from that shop across the street while you wait?"

Filmore rolled his eyes. "The shop is called Sadie's. Owned by the Garrison family, the building has been a landmark in Belclare since the town was founded."

"Good to know." He looked past Filmore to the kid behind the desk. Riley pegged him as early twenties and fresh out of the academy. "How about you, Officer?"

"Call me Danny." The young cop grinned, relief stamped on his face. "I'll take a hot chocolate."

"All right. Marshmallows or whipped cream? Cinnamon on top?"

"Sounds like you've been to Sadie's before," Danny said knowingly.

Riley shrugged into his down vest. "A man who doesn't cook has priorities."

The cop's expression brightened more, making him look even younger. Riley was grateful to gain an ally in town, even a young one. Since getting hired on, he'd learned that people here were a bit edgy around strangers. The guys on the crew who'd worked previous seasons said it wasn't normal for Belclare, but they all agreed the folks had good reason. The national news headlining drug bust marked the first serious crime in their community and they were worried that more would follow.

"I take marshmallows," Danny said. "No cinnamon."

"Good choice," Riley smiled. "How about you?" he asked the older man again. "Last chance."

"No," Filmore snapped. "Thank you. I am capable of fetching my own coffee."

Riley paused, one hand on the door. "The girl at the counter said they were doing some sugar-cookie thing this afternoon. What's that about?"

Danny sighed wistfully. "I asked for the time off but didn't get it."

Filmore glared at the kid. "You cannot convince me the

police department puts safety first when our officers are more concerned with a sugar-cookie party."

"It's a big deal," Danny defended himself.

Filmore launched right into another snobby rant, complaints and insults flying like fists.

Riley was about to intervene with another dumb new-guy-in-town question when a harsh, earsplitting whistle silenced the argument.

All three men in the lobby turned to the woman in the doorway that led back to the bull pen.

The woman of the hour, Riley decided, soaking up his first live view of Police Chief Jensen. Her blond hair was pulled back from her heart-shaped face and her blue eyes were sharp as lasers as she studied each of them.

Unlike the other officers he'd seen coming and going today, she wasn't wearing the dark blue uniform. No, she wore a deep green suit with an ivory shirt, tailored perfectly to her curves. Was it some attempt at a civilian disguise or didn't she lead by example? He took in her slender legs and the high heels and decided he appreciated the view too much to criticize her choice or rationale. Were police chiefs supposed to wear skirts? He knew the formal uniforms for women were that way, but on an average day? He'd seen her on television, had researched the decorated career that led to her current post. None of it accurately portrayed the size of her personal presence. She might be a petite little thing, but without saying a word she had full command of the room.

Her hard gaze moved deliberately from Danny to Filmore to him. He felt it like a touch. After a moment, she settled that tough blue gaze back on Filmore.

"Mr. Filmore, what is the problem here?"

"I need a moment of your time," he began. "The new precautions are an impediment—"

She held up a hand and he stopped talking. Riley put that skill right up there with a superpower. One fact had been immediately clear: the president of the historical society loved the sound of his own voice.

Her cool gaze landed on Riley again, raked him from head to toe and back up. "You are?"

"Not a part of this," he said, holding up his hands. "I'm just on garland detail." He pointed to the ladder.

She eyed the ladder and then stepped forward, holding out a hand. "Name and identification, please."

He hoped this was a stunt for the crotchety Filmore. "Was I hanging garland too fast, ma'am?"

She glared at him.

"I checked his credentials when he came in, Chief," Danny piped up. "He's with the design team."

"Your name," she insisted.

Riley gave her his friendliest lopsided grin. "Riley O'Brien." The grin didn't appear to be any more effective on the police chief than when he'd used it on his teachers in private school.

"You're Irish?"

"That's what my parents tell me." According to his new background courtesy of the Specialists' technology wizards, he was first-generation American, born of Irish immigrants. As he'd memorized his manufactured past it was as if the techs had somehow tapped the childhood fantasy that carried him through his long years at the orphanage.

"What brings you to Belclare?"

"Steady work," he replied as she returned his Maryland driver's license and the work permit.

"And you'll be leaving when?"

"Actually, I'm thinking I'll stay." He looked over to Danny. "Maybe you can point me to a place to rent?"

"The personnel don't typically stay on after the work is done," the chief countered before Danny could reply.

Riley shrugged. "So far, I like what I see."

She examined his progress with the decorations. "Why aren't you done?"

"I was taking my required break, but that got interrupted."

"Well, we won't waste any more of your time."

"Thank you." He returned his wallet to his back pocket and zipped up his vest halfway. With a wave to Danny, he headed out to Sadie's while the chief addressed Mr. Filmore.

The sky was heavy and he smelled snow on the air. Riley didn't need a weather forecast to tell him Belclare's annual Christmas Village would benefit from an idyllic blanket of fluffy white snow for the opening weekend. The most profitable weekend according to the background reports. All he had to do was make sure no one ruined it for them by assassinating their beloved chief of police.

Sadie's was quiet and the hot chocolate orders were ready sooner than he'd hoped. He needed to keep an eye on the chief, but he also wanted a few minutes of distance to gather his thoughts. Whatever he'd expected, she'd been... more. Sure, she was beautiful and she clearly had her finger on the pulse of this town. He didn't like how that made him feel. Uneasy. Turned-on. A potential lifelong assignment out here suddenly took on a new element of risk. And a potential unexpected angle.

What if he asked her out? It would be a valid way to stay close, especially in these early days. He headed back over to the police station, planning how best to get a few details about her out of Danny. Riley knew how to ask questions without giving away his real motives.

Work, he reminded himself. That was his real motive. This wasn't the time to get distracted.

Chapter Two

"You simply must relax the police presence on Main," Mr. Filmore said, not for the first time.

Too bad Abby didn't have any evidence tying him to any illegal activity. Not even a whiff of mental instability or aggression in his background.

As much as Filmore tested her patience, she refused to give in to the temptation to play favorites. All the citizens of Belclare deserved her best effort as their police chief. It was a shame she didn't trust them equally anymore.

Despite the press conference that had gone viral thanks to national news and social media, in recent days her confident speech felt more like a publicity stunt. She knew the value of perception as well as caution. The mail and email that flooded the department and website in the days following the drug bust was mostly positive, but the threats, in an increasing number, had to be assessed and cleared or sent up to the feds, who claimed she was in trouble. They'd even suggested she employ a protective detail, but they hadn't given her the personnel. Besides, with everyone in town watching for her next mistake, she had enough eyes on her already.

The threats monopolized her time, taking her away from other important daily endeavors, though Homeland Security would disagree with that assessment. They were sure she was dealing with a sleeper cell and their insistence, while absurd, had her looking at everyone in town with suspicion. She knew these people. Cared about them—even the hardheaded one glaring at her right now.

Of course, Martin didn't care that she'd drawn that line with his safety in mind. Aesthetics and historical accuracy mattered more than anything else to him. Thankfully, the men and women on the police force agreed with the aggressive line she'd drawn.

"I will not relax the patrols on Main or anywhere else, Mr. Filmore."

"But the problem was out at the docks. Isn't it a better use of resources to keep your patrols focused in that area?"

He wanted her to save resources in the hope that he could divert any funds she didn't spend into his budget at the next council meeting. She knew the tactic far too well. She'd taken this job despite the politics that went with it. Abby felt the tension mounting. Her shoulders were tight, her legs were ready to spring and her toes were cramping in these stupid pumps. She reminded herself she couldn't throw a tantrum. There were better outlets than the blood-curdling scream of frustration trapped in her throat.

A soft tap-tap-tap of a hammer and squeak of boots on the metal ladder told her O'Brien was back to work in the lobby. Talk about an outlet. Wow. Riley O'Brien would certainly qualify as an effective distraction. He was handsome and built. If only she could be sure he wasn't also a threat in contractor's clothing. Had she really just thought that? She gave herself a mental shake. This had to be some universal female fantasy involving a thermal shirt, faded jeans and a tool belt that sparked sudden, inexplicable lust in a stranger under present circumstances.

"Well?" Filmore demanded.

She dragged herself back to the present. Mr. Filmore

deserved a thoughtful reply. "I could have the increased patrols work in their civilian clothes."

"How is that any better?"

She knew it! It wasn't about the official uniform presence hindering anything. His dissatisfaction was about the budget. She was done with Filmore's whining and she had another appointment in just fifteen minutes. Abby squared her shoulders. "My officers will be out there, in uniform. End of discussion. They will not harass anyone, because I've given clear instructions—" based on the most recent threats that she didn't bother explaining "—regarding what they should look for."

Filmore made an unpleasant sound of frustration. "I suppose you expect me to be grateful."

She smiled, remembering he was a decent guy if a bit uptight about historical accuracy. "I expect you to recognize the necessity of the situation. Together is the only way Belclare gets through this rough patch."

His beady eyes locked on to her. "You might have thought of this 'rough patch' before you turned our town into a target."

Before she could respond, he spun on his heel and marched out of her office, his spine ramrod straight.

Abby let him have the last word. Not because he deserved it, but because she refused to be late to her next appointment. She was ready for a bit of solitude in her car and the comfort of coffee and conversation with a friend who didn't have an agenda. She shut down her computer and moved away from her desk. Adjusting the silk scarf at her throat, she slipped into her black wool overcoat.

She was debating the wisdom of ruining her look by switching from her heels to her winter boots when someone knocked on her office door. Again. She turned and the professional smile she'd forced onto her face faded at the sight of Riley O'Brien filling her doorway. "Yes?"

"Danny said I could come on back."

She made a mental note to have a chat with Danny.

"I just wanted you to know I'd finished the lobby as well as the display out front."

"I'm sure your boss will be thrilled with your efficiency."

"Probably so." He gave her a grin that reminded her of the young men she'd pulled over in the past who tried to get off with a warning. "Today's project list filled two pages."

"That's…" Why did he think she cared? "Ambitious," she finished. "If you'll excuse me I have an appointment."

"Oh, sure." He stepped out of the doorway but hovered while she locked up. It was a new procedure and no reflection on her department but—

"Can't be too careful these days," he said, echoing her thoughts.

"Precisely." She maneuvered around him, unable to ignore the enticing scent of evergreen and cinnamon clinging to his clothing. "The garland is scented this year? I didn't approve that."

"I'm not sure it's possible to un-scent fresh pine, ma'am."

"Stop that."

"Stop what?"

"The ma'am thing. I don't like it much." It made her feel old and right now the increased pressure following the drug bust was more than enough to cope with.

"Right." He shoved his hands deep into his pockets. "Danny mentioned that."

She was definitely having a talk with Danny. He needed a reminder about basic security around strangers. "Enjoy your stay in Belclare, Mr. O'Brien."

"Call me Riley."

Abby had no intention of calling him anything at all.

While it wouldn't be a problem under normal circumstances, this wasn't the best time to make new friends. Except when she looked up, his expression was open and there was a humor lurking in his brown eyes. Her earlier thoughts about a stress relief outlet flooded back.

"I'd like that."

"Pardon?" In her fantasy, she'd apparently lost the thread of the conversation. Reaching into her pocket, she gripped her car keys and strode toward the back of the station. He followed her.

"I'd like to enjoy my stay. If you're not doing anything tonight, maybe you could show me around?"

Startled, she stopped, gathered her foolishly scattered wits. "I'm the chief of police, Mr.—" she made the correction before he could "—*Riley*. If you need a map or a tour guide, check with the Visitor's Center."

"I don't get it." He shook his head.

She shouldn't ask. If she let him stall her much longer, she'd be late. "What's the matter?"

He grinned again. "I thought we sort of, well, connected earlier."

"You're joking." The idea was absurd.

"Only a little." His eyes twinkled. "Call it instant hero worship instead of a connection. I didn't think anything could make Mr. Filmore stop talking."

The urge to laugh startled her and she smothered it quickly. "That was more luck than skill." A distaste for Filmore's voice was a connection shared by 90 percent of Belclare's population. "I really need to go."

"Okay." He pushed open the door and held it for her. "If you change your mind or need anything decorated, I'll be around."

His slow smile and the warmth of his body as she brushed by him created a stir low in her belly. Simple lust.

A tempting distraction she couldn't risk at the moment, no matter how genuine he seemed or how efficiently he tacked up decorations. The cold air slipped around her legs and up her knee-length skirt. She was rather grateful for the assist from Mother Nature as parts of her had turned inappropriately warm during this bizarre conversation. "You'll be around? For the month?"

"Longer, I think. I like the views," he added, his gaze holding hers. "Better get going before you catch a chill."

Right. If only her feet weren't rooted to the spot.

As he pulled the door closed, she brought out her key to lock it. "Don't worry. I'll get it from this side. Danny told me all doors had to be locked at all times."

She clamped her lips together. No sense hollering at the new guy for the mistakes of the rookie cop at the desk. "Thank you," she murmured when the door latch clicked. She counted to ten, then tugged the handle, pleased when the lock held.

She hurried to her car. At least the new guy in town kept his word about the little things. Even that small assurance immediately put her in a better frame of mind as she drove out to her meeting with Belclare's most reluctant celebrity, Deke Maynard.

Quiet, reserved and a gifted artist, Deke had become a true friend. Aside from his assistant, she was probably the only person in town he trusted. She appreciated that and after all the recent criticism, she valued the few people like Deke who supported her. Keeping to their weekly routine of coffee and conversation in his elegant home gave her hope things would soon return to normal in Belclare and made her feel like more than just the chief.

Nothing wrong with wanting to feel like a woman now and again. Didn't have to mean anything. She thought of the handsome new stranger in town and shook her head.

The dead last thing she needed was another complication in her life.

Maybe she'd better stick with just being the chief.

Chapter Three

Standing at the wall of windows on the east side of the room he'd converted into a painting studio, Deke Maynard stared out over the sleepy town of Belclare. Three years ago he'd visited during their annual Christmas Village and declared himself enamored with the charm, views and people.

He'd purchased this house and established himself as a recluse during the remodeling. Oh, he wandered out occasionally and spoke with people, but it was all he could do not to laugh in the eager faces of the ignorant citizens of Belclare as they gladly accommodated his every whim and eccentricity.

He should have asked for hazard pay when he'd agreed to create his base of operations here. The day-to-day tedium of Belclare might kill him. Yet there were certain perks, he admitted to himself as the police chief's car turned into his long driveway.

The woman was beautiful and intelligent. If he bothered with regrets, he might have second thoughts about the things he'd set in motion. As it was, he scolded himself for entertaining the idea of keeping her as a trophy. It was a risk the operation could not afford.

"Chief Jensen has arrived, sir," his assistant reported after a quick rap on the studio door.

"Thank you," he said, as though he wasn't watching her approach.

The reports from town annoyed him. She'd doubled patrols everywhere. Quite a feat considering the limits of her staff, but if nothing else, they were a determined and loyal flock of sheep.

He was reluctantly impressed that she'd managed to make the drug bust at all. That had been pure police work. There had been no leaks in the chain of information. When he'd arrived and become acquainted with her, he'd considered her more of a decorative figurehead than a real cop. He'd mistakenly assumed she'd been named police chief out of some misguided attempt to appeal to those who clamored for equality.

Looking back, he was grateful he'd been diligent about his manufactured background or today's meeting might be taking an entirely different and unpleasant turn.

The doorbell rang and Deke smiled to himself. His assistant would manage the door and get her settled with coffee. Then Deke could make his entrance as the eccentric artist she expected.

Appreciating her strengths didn't change the fact that Chief Jensen had become enemy number one. As the town dressed itself for their penultimate tourist season, Deke had been making his own preparations. He weighed the pros and cons of his limited choices.

In a matter of weeks, Chief Jensen had single-handedly wrecked a strategy years in the making. If he didn't act swiftly to rectify the situation, his reputation would be ruined beyond repair.

He examined the landscape on the canvas in front of him. His raw artistic talent would never carry him as far as his other skills. Skills powerful men and organizations paid handsomely for.

Wiping the paint from his hands, he checked his appearance in the mirror at the top of the stairs before he descended to meet the police chief. This would be one of his most critical performances to date. And with all good performances, it would be better for tapping into the truth.

Her drug bust might have cut off a vital money supply line, but that didn't change his base, physical attraction to her. It would be that truth he monopolized today for the greater good of his real career.

Pausing at the landing, he took one last deep breath before rushing the rest of the way down the stairs. "Ah, Abby, hello," he said as he entered the sitting room just off the foyer. "Forgive me for keeping you waiting."

Chief Jensen smiled brightly as she stood to greet him. "You could've rescheduled if you're working."

"Nonsense. Coffee with you is the highlight of my week." That put a rosy glow in her cheeks. He stepped back to admire her. "You are looking as lovely as ever."

"Thank you."

He motioned for her to resume her seat, then he poured a cup of coffee for himself. "So how are the preparations going? From my vantage point it seems everything is on schedule."

"You should come down and take a look for yourself," she suggested, a soft smile on her lips.

He was filled once more with the urge to keep her. He deserved a reward for the nonsense he tolerated day in and day out. "Right now I'd only be in the way. I'll come down after the crush of opening weekend is over."

"I'll look forward to it." She raised the china cup to her full lips and he had to look away. "The mayor came by the station yesterday."

"Oh?" he queried.

"Yes. He wanted me to thank you for the sketches you donated to the silent auction."

"Of course he had you bring me the message." Deke snorted derisively and adjusted his rolled-back sleeves, pleased to see her watching him so closely. "He knew I wouldn't let him past the driveway after the way he spoke to you."

"Probably," she allowed. "Thanks again for defending me."

"You're a hero," he said. "And you're a dear friend," he added quietly. He checked the time, wondering how far he could push her today.

"To be fair, I might have shown a little restraint at the press conference." She held up her hand, thumb and finger close together. "Maybe a smidge less gloating."

"That drug bust was important." Deke leaned forward and laid a hand on her knee. It wasn't the first time he'd touched her, but this time he wanted her to understand it was a romantic advance. "You're a passionate woman." Her eyes widened and he knew he had her on the hook. "Belclare is fortunate that you're putting fear and doubt into the minds of criminals looking to abuse our resources."

He sat back once more, his hand trailing away slowly, giving her the impression that the next move was hers. He'd long ago learned how to manipulate and guide while maintaining the illusion of free will.

She cleared her throat. "I was surprised to see you at the emergency council meeting."

"Should I have stayed home?"

"No." Her brow furrowed for a moment before her expression cleared. "Your defense meant the world to me. Frankly, after the mayor's reprimand, I didn't expect anyone to admit I existed. Your example reminds me I do have allies."

She's made her decision. He could sense victory on the horizon. That moment, when she was his, would be so sweet. His body responded, anticipating the pleasure of using her before he publicly humiliated and destroyed her. In a few days' time her world would come crashing down around her. He glanced at the clock on the mantel. "Then I'm even happier to have made the effort."

"You've been an asset to the entire community." Whatever she intended to say next was cut short by the hum of her phone. "Excuse me, it's the station."

"Of course," he said with a nonchalance he didn't feel. This might be the very call that signaled the beginning of his vengeance.

He refilled his coffee and waited while she took the call in the foyer. He didn't hear much beyond her greeting before his own phone rang. The timing couldn't be worse, but he answered anyway. "Yes?"

"This is a mistake," the caller said with a quaking voice.

"The only mistake is questioning me."

"I was told I had the authority—"

"Enough." Deke checked to be sure Chief Jensen remained distracted. "When you exhibit good judgment your authority will be restored. Are you reneging on our solution?"

"N-n-no," the voice on the other end of the line stuttered.

"Good." Deke ended the call and tucked his phone back into his pocket.

"Deke?"

"Yes, my dear," he said, coming to his feet. "Don't tell me duty calls." She'd already taken her overcoat from the hall tree.

"Something like that." She hesitated, her bold, blue gaze roaming over his face. "Thank you for the coffee, Deke."

He stepped forward, taking her coat to help her into it.

He let his hands brush the soft skin at her nape as he adjusted the collar, smiling to himself when she trembled.

"Let's not wait a week," he said. "Come back for dinner tomorrow night."

She turned, and he took great pleasure watching her face as all of her responsibilities went to war against the desire he'd carefully stoked. "I would like that," she replied.

"But?"

Her mouth tipped down, heavy with regret. "I have a security update tomorrow night."

"Stop by after. I'll show you my latest seascape," he said, hoping she'd laugh.

She did. "I know you better than that."

"I would like you to," he said, raising her hands to his lips.

She took a small step back, her eyes wide.

He cursed himself for pushing too hard, but he had a schedule to keep.

"I'll call you when my meeting is done tomorrow." She paused at the door. "Then you can let me know if I should stop by or if it's too late."

He knew she wasn't referring to the time. Again, she impressed him by understanding the little nuances. If only more of the men he worked with were as astute.

As he closed the door behind her he let himself enjoy another heady rush of anticipation. As angry as he was that she'd busted a drug shipment his clients relied on, she deserved respect. When she came by after her meeting everything would be different. She would be in pain over the blow he was about to inflict on her precious Belclare and he would be the only one able to soothe her. Tomorrow night, his plans would be in full swing and his reputation preserved.

He watched from the sidelight window as she drove

away. She made him angry, yes, but he liked her. He could send a message to others and still preserve the idealism that made her so unique. Silently he vowed that she wouldn't live to know how badly she'd misjudged him.

It was the only courtesy he could afford when it came to Chief Abby Jensen.

Chapter Four

Abby left Deke's house, almost grateful to be called to a vandalism scene at the town limit. When he touched her, she couldn't decide how to feel about it. Maybe because he didn't touch her often enough? She was starting to wonder if anyone would ever touch her enough.

She wasn't sure about the answer, which only annoyed her. When they'd started these weekly coffee meetings it had been a way for her to keep tabs on the enigmatic and cloistered resident of Belclare. Now, though, the truth was far more embarrassing.

For months, she'd been fighting her attraction to the man. He was in his mid-forties, but the gray at his temples and his artistic worldview only made him more distinguished in her eyes. The flawless manners, superb taste and maturity didn't hurt, either.

He treated her as if she was someone special and she liked the idea that at least one person saw beyond her badge and title to the woman underneath. She liked to think of herself as more than a uniform dedicated to maintaining law and order.

"So you've been taking a weekly coffee break for the ego boost," she muttered, drumming her fingertips on her steering wheel. Even in solitude that sounded pretty pathetic.

Except it had felt anything but pathetic when he'd called

her passionate. And that invite to dinner…was he heading where he seemed to be heading?

"You're flattered," she said, coaching herself right out of the potential romance of it. She hadn't had much of a social life since taking the top post in the Belclare police department, hesitant to set herself up for idle gossip. "Get over yourself. The positive attention is nice, but you can't afford the distraction."

As if on cue, her cell phone launched into "I Fought the Law," the ringtone she'd programmed for business calls. She toggled the button on her steering wheel to answer. "Chief Jensen."

"Hi, Chief. It's Danny."

"I'm ten minutes away."

"Right. It's just…"

She waited. He cleared his throat as worst-case scenarios danced at the edge of her mind. She would not entertain those unless and until facts forced her to do so.

Her personal life might be a haze of self-doubt and bad timing, but her career had been marked with success every step of the way. Her work ethic, common sense and focus had served her well and she wasn't about to toss those strengths out the window.

"Spit it out, Danny."

"The responding officers want you to know the media is already on-site."

Damn it. "Thanks for the heads-up." She appreciated the warning. If the media was on-site, then Mayor Scott wouldn't be far behind. Now she was doubly grateful for choosing the suit and heels today. In her opinion, her suits made her more relatable than the uniform, especially after her hard-nosed speech had become a viral internet sensation.

As she approached the scene, she cringed at the growing crowd. Good grief. If she'd just heard, how had a news crew from Baltimore arrived so quickly? Her officers were pushing people back, but that only gave the media a better overall shot for tonight's headlines.

It looked worse in person than it had on her phone. The Welcome to Belclare display had been altered with spray paint. The phrases "Death to Chief Jensen" and "Open season on Belclare" were now blotting out points of town pride.

The threats weren't new, but they'd been out of the public eye. This...*this* was bold and obvious. It was a challenge she couldn't ignore. "Open season on Belclare" required a careful, strategic response. How had whoever was responsible for this pulled it off without getting caught?

A reporter shoved a microphone in front of her as she went to join the responding officers. "Chief, what's your reaction to such personal threats?"

She pushed her clenched fists deeper into her coat pockets. "The childish vandal responsible for this negative display will be found and dealt with."

"Are there any security cameras out here that might have caught the vandal?"

Abby kept walking, refusing to acknowledge the silly question. There was a Christmas tree lot just around the next bend and nothing but trees until the sign. "If you'll excuse me, I need to speak with my officers." She ducked under the tape the responding officers had used to block the immediate area.

Reporters shouted at her back.

"Should the citizens of Belclare be taking more defensive action?"

"Will you shut down the city?"

"Will the Christmas Village be canceled?"

She couldn't let that one go. She turned, ready to answer when the mayor's voice rang out through the crisp winter air.

"This small attempt to interrupt our annual traditions is hardly cause for alarm."

Abby couldn't believe he was taking her side. *About time,* she thought.

"Chief Jensen's—" he hesitated for three seconds "—*enthusiasm* has obviously created a few unpleasant ripples, but Belclare is strong and united, and determined to make this the best holiday season ever. We look forward to seeing all of you this weekend."

Abby found herself fighting a sudden urge to silence Mayor Scott. She banished the compulsion. He was better in the media spotlight and, whether or not he believed her or agreed with her methods, ultimately they were working toward the same goal: a safe community and a safe holiday event.

She let him ramble on giving the proper sound bites that likely included a subtle invitation for other criminal justice professionals to apply for her job.

"Do we have anything?" Abby ignored her chilled feet as she listened to her officers explain what they'd found. Or rather what they hadn't found.

"One of the vendors coming in for the weekend reported it," said Officer Gadsden.

"Did you get a statement?"

"We did, so it helps set a time frame for the vandals."

She stepped closer, pressed her finger to a dripping streak of paint. "Still tacky. Someone had fun during their lunch hour." She looked to the ground. "Any hope for shoe prints?"

"No." Officer Gadsden knelt down and Abby followed suit. "The snow's been trampled by more than one person. Right back to the road."

"Great." Abby wanted to clean this up herself, right this minute. "See what you can get off any traffic cameras between here and Baltimore. And ask around Sadie's and other restaurants. Maybe the vandals came into town for lunch."

"You got it."

She covered her mouth with her hand, unwilling to risk anyone in the media reading her lips. "As you take pictures, get the bystanders." It wasn't unusual for vandals of this sort to hang around to watch the cops scramble for answers.

"Chief Jensen!"

She turned slowly, unable to ignore the mayor's shout. "Yes?" It was a small measure of relief that he remained on the other side of the tape. For her, the shock was seeing him alone. Victor Scott loved his entourage, whether it was his hired staff or an impromptu gathering of media professionals.

He waved her closer and she did her best to hide her distaste at the arrogant summons. Mayor Scott enjoyed the political posturing, but playing along was her least favorite, necessary part of the job. She preferred a straightforward exchange. Less chance for mixed signals or missed goals that way.

"How long until you have this cleaned up?" he demanded with his practiced concerned frown in place.

"The sign or the crime?"

"You can't manage both?"

"Repairing the sign isn't exactly police responsibility," she said, clinging to her last shred of composure. "As for the vandal—" she glanced back at the damage "—we believe there was more than one person involved. There are databases with graffiti signatures and tags—"

"This criminal signed his work?" the mayor exclaimed too loudly.

"We're not sure yet. That's part of the problem. Or the solution," she added, just to give him something else to focus on. "As for the sign itself, once we have our pictures it can be repainted and repaired right away."

"No! Nooo!"

Abby and the mayor swiveled toward the pitiful wail of Mr. Filmore. When Mayor Scott rolled his eyes, she realized they shared a mutual frustration with the historical society president. It was strangely affirming.

"What now, Filmore?" With a hand on Filmore's shoulder, the mayor stopped him from barreling into the crime scene.

"You can't just *paint* that sign."

"We can't just leave it," the mayor shot back.

Abby glanced at her officers, grateful they were snapping pictures of everything and everyone as she'd asked and not laughing aloud at the ridiculous debate.

"This gateway to Belclare has been meticulously maintained for over one hundred and eighty years. It must be cleaned, not merely slapped at with another coat of paint."

The mayor loomed over the skinny frame of Filmore. "I am not allowing those threats to remain visible any longer than necessary. Get a team out here if you must but get it handled immediately."

For once, Abby was grateful for Filmore's presence. The man's shrill insistence about preservation diverted the mayor's attention from her.

She used the time and space to take her own inventory of faces in the crowd. She recognized reporters and television station logos. More than a few people from town had followed the noise and commotion to come take a look. She felt the collective irritation from those business owners whose praise for her drug bust quickly turned to criticism after her speech garnered national attention.

She returned to her officers. "Keep the area secure. Do we have anything to cover it in the short term?"

"I have a tarp in my car."

She nodded. "It's a start." Pointing to the camera Gadsden was using, she asked, "Is anyone standing out to you?"

He shook his head. "No one seems too proud of themselves. Except the mayor."

She chuckled. "I'm sure he has photo evidence of his whereabouts for the entire morning."

"Our chances of catching the vandals and making an arrest are pretty slim."

"All we can do is our best." She pulled her car keys from her pocket. "I'll find someone to babysit the sign." Her department was stretched too thin already, but she refused to allow a repeat performance.

"We could put up a couple of motion-activated cameras," Gadsden offered.

"With this circus watching?" She shook her head. "I like the idea but the vandals would only come back and hit those first." She scanned the faces on the other side of the road again. It was a valid idea, if they could find a window when no one else was around. Too late to contain the media, she knew Belclare residents would be upset with her all over again. "Let's talk about it at the station when we have more than the nothing we have now."

Gadsden agreed and Abby headed back to her car, giving appropriate sound bites to the media on the way. She wanted the quiet of her office and some heat for her freezing feet. Unfortunately, she was blocked in by a dark blue pickup truck she didn't recognize.

It had to belong to one of the temporary workers or vendors. She stifled the urge to look back at the death threat on the sign. She would not let some silly stunt likely staged by a teenager with too much idle time and a bad sense of humor get under her skin. Paranoia was neither professional nor helpful.

"Excuse me, Chief Jensen."

A car door slammed with a bang and, despite her best effort, her body jerked, braced for an attack.

"Didn't mean to startle you."

Abby surveyed the tall stranger who seemed determined to show up in her life today. And he *had* startled her. Denying it would be foolish. "No problem. Mr. O'Brien, isn't it?"

"That would be my father," he said with a softer smile that did strange things to her pulse. "I'm just Riley, remember?" He leaned against the pickup's door. "I heard the breaking news on the way out." His brown eyes were taking in the ugly scene behind her. "Any leads?"

She tucked her hands back into her pockets. "I could have sworn you told me you had steady work. Why are you insinuating yourself into mine?"

"I'll take that as a no. And I'd be working if my next job wasn't taped off."

She gave in and rubbed at the tension in her neck. Hadn't there been a time when Belclare folks had just done their own thing without professional design teams and small armies of temporary workers? She missed those days. Of course, with the way the Christmas Village had grown it was impossible to set up without help. While everyone liked how December brought a wealth of tourists into town, the police department maintained a higher alert for petty crimes.

Since she'd taken over, the worst they'd dealt with had been a string of burglaries and one car theft. The burglaries had been teenagers looking for trouble and all of the stolen items had been recovered and returned. The car theft had been a pair of temporary workers operating under the influence of alcohol and stupidity.

Yeah, those were the days.

This year, she had legitimate concerns about how to protect Belclare effectively. There wasn't enough time or manpower to run background checks on every new person in town. Her meetings with business owners hadn't gone well, most of them siding with the mayor that the additional threats were her problem to solve since she'd brought it on them.

At some point in Belclare's past, the police chief would have been hailed as a hero for that bust for more than a few hours. But despite the public resentment and doubt, she understood the financial importance of the upcoming days and she was doing her best to make sure it all came together without any further tragedy.

The ugly vandalism didn't bode well.

"Until Mr. Filmore decides how to proceed with the cleanup, this area is off-limits."

"I'll let my boss know." He pulled a cell phone out of the pocket of his dark red vest.

She frowned. "Don't you own a real coat?"

"Sure." He gave her a strange look. "It gets in the way when I'm working."

"I see."

"Don't worry. I won't die of frostbite on you."

Based on the way her body reacted to him, frostbite wasn't a concern for her, either, if he was nearby. She'd nearly forgotten about her freezing feet during this unexpected conversation. She glared back at the sign. "No one is going to die of anything around here."

"Glad to hear it," he said, his attention on his phone.

"Could you move your truck, please? I have things to do and you're blocking me in."

"Sure." With the phone to his ear, he settled into the

driver's seat. His voice was a low rumble as he explained the problem to his boss.

Then the engine masked his conversation as he rolled out of the way, giving her a small wave.

In her own car, she cranked up the heat and hit shuffle on her iPod, letting the blast of AC/DC fill the car on her way through town. She needed the loud, demanding beat to blot out her thoughts. There was no point in doubting her course of action. She wouldn't take back the words even if she could. As her thoughts cycled, she spotted Riley's truck about a block behind her.

He wasn't following her. That would be paranoid, fearful thinking and she wouldn't give in to it. She wouldn't sink to the level that gave some rumored local terrorists the advantage. He was headed for one of the warehouses down by the docks and this was the most direct route through town. But he turned when she did, heading north away from Main Street, directly opposite the route to the docks.

She practiced it in her mind, running through her defensive options as he continued to tail her. Preparation wasn't paranoia, she assured herself.

Abby nearly cracked when he was practically on her bumper as she turned onto her street. She debated driving right by her house, but decided her address was no secret and it was time to make a stand. With that thought echoing in her brain, she pulled into her driveway.

But Riley didn't pull in behind her; he pulled into the driveway right beside hers. In fact, the way the two homes were situated, they were now parked side by side.

What the hell? All concept of her attraction to the man vanished instantly. He was like a bad penny turning up everywhere today. The house next door had been vacant for several weeks, since Mr. and Mrs. Hamilton had gone to Florida to visit their grandchildren. He had no business being on her street or in their driveway.

She yanked her purse from the passenger seat and got out of the car. "What do you think you're doing, Mr. O'Brien?"

Chapter Five

"Hey, Chief." Riley tipped his head in greeting, his expression easy. "Call me Riley," he reminded her. He shrugged. "The boss told me to try again first thing tomorrow. No sense unloading tonight just to load it up again in the morning."

She rounded the hood of her car, one hand in her purse on the grip of her gun. "That doesn't explain why you're following me."

"Following you?" He glanced at the two vehicles as if just noticing they were parked next to each other. "No such luck. I just came on home."

"Home?"

"Well, at least home for now. I signed the rental agreement during my lunch break."

"The Hamiltons didn't say anything about renting out their house."

He shrugged. "I wouldn't know. I've never met them."

"Never met?" she echoed. "But that's their house." Exasperated, she stepped forward. "I need some sort of proof of your claim, Mr. O'Brien."

He raised his hands like he was surrendering. "Take it easy. Let me get the paperwork."

This was intolerable. He couldn't be her neighbor. She couldn't cope with having a stranger living so close. Not right now when she saw a potential threat in the faces of people she'd known for years. Okay, so maybe it was more than the easygoing attitude and absolute raw sex appeal. While neither of those traits had ever ranked high on her list of trustworthy features, Riley affected her differently. At precisely the time when she needed to trust herself, life dumped this hunk of handsomeness and doubt right next door.

Frustrated, she hastily flipped through the folder he handed her. The letterhead was familiar, as was the Realtor's name. The lease agreement and signatures all seemed to be in order.

"She should have told me," Abby muttered.

"I told you I liked your town."

"That hardly validates renting a house."

"Are you always this anxious when someone moves in?"

The question seized her attention, forced her to think like a cop rather than a frightened victim trapped in the crosshairs of a rifle she couldn't see. "No. No," she repeated as the day suddenly caught up with her. She handed him the folder. "My apologies. It's been a little dicey around here lately. I'm surprised the realty company didn't warn you off. I thought everyone believed I was a magnet for trouble."

"They did mention it actually."

She laughed. The sound was laced with a bit of weary hysteria, but it felt pretty good anyway. "So you're looking for trouble?"

RILEY TOSSED THE paperwork back into the cab and stuffed his hands into his pockets. He almost felt bad that he couldn't tell the woman the truth, but breaking cover wasn't the answer. "I'm not looking for trouble, just work." He glanced to the house. "And anywhere that isn't a hotel room, really."

"That lease is for a year," she said.

He watched her shifting, rubbing her legs together a bit. She was cold but too stubborn to take care of herself until she knew if he was friend or foe. Based on the threats aimed her way, he figured that showed remarkable determination and a hefty dose of intelligence.

"The Realtor approached me while I was decorating their building. When I learned the owners wanted some work done and ideas for a remodel, I knew this was the right place for me." Again he was grateful for the deep background and work history Director Casey had created for him. The proximity to the chief simplified his surveillance plans.

"Welcome to the neighborhood," she said with obvious reluctance. She stuck out her gloved hand.

He accepted the gesture. Her hand felt small in his, but there was strength in the grip. He wanted to ask what kind of weapon she preferred. The woman oozed tough under the contrasting layers of wariness and the feminine heels and power suit. She was a puzzle he wanted to solve, but he suspected he wouldn't get anywhere by pushing her.

"You'd better get inside and warm up," he said, releasing her hand and closing his truck door. "If you need anything, just come on over."

"Right. Same goes."

"Thanks." When she walked away, he turned for his own front door.

"A word of warning, Riley."

"Yeah?"

"Mrs. Wilks will probably be down with a plate of cookies."

"That doesn't sound so awful."

"Exactly. Her cookies are addictive, you'll see." Her smile changed everything about her face. It chased away the worry and brightened those blue eyes. It gave him a glimpse of what she was like without the cloud of stress over her head. "It's why we all put up with her benign nosiness."

"Got it."

With a nod, she pushed open her front door and disappeared.

He walked around the truck and up the path, entering the front door of his house wondering what the hell to do now. When they'd left the vandalized sign, he'd hoped she'd go to the police station so he could take a quick walk through her house.

Light flirting hadn't worked at the station and just now she'd barely accepted him being neighborly. He had to find a way to keep an eye on her without driving her out of his sight while he searched for an imminent threat. From what he'd heard around town, everyone was at least irritated with her if not outright angry. It made it tough to sort out who was hiding the terrorist tendencies.

He walked straight back to the kitchen and put his vest on the peg by the back door. The simple act had him recalling the chief's concern about his coat. One more piece of the developing picture that was her. Could he use that innate concern to his advantage?

He glanced out the side window, across their mirrored driveways, to her house. Resigned, he pulled a beer from the refrigerator, leaned back against the counter and contemplated the Hamiltons' outdated kitchen.

His tape measure was on his tool belt in the truck, but he paced off the flooring and started mulling over the cost and benefits of tile versus vinyl. Reclaimed hardwood might be an option, too. The space wasn't too big. But the weather could make tracking down those materials a challenge. Per his agreement, any changes beyond basic repair would need to be approved.

Oh, well, he wasn't in a rush. There was plenty of re-modeling to keep him busy and maintain his cover even after he was done with the holiday setup. He rolled some of the ache from his shoulders. The physical work would give his brain time to sort out the people who were ready to act on their anger toward the chief.

He'd only been in town a couple of days and it wasn't a stretch that criminals thought they could slip under the radar in this sleepy little waterside town. Chief Jensen had things under control, but the police force was small, as was the community. The docks did brisk business and the smaller port meant quicker turnaround, which meant ship-ments didn't linger long enough to get caught.

Riley walked into the den where he'd tucked his laptop into the small writing desk. The Hamiltons' decorating style wasn't exactly his taste, but the privacy and security beat a motel.

He turned on the television and found a music channel for background noise, then sat down to review everything he could find about Belclare, working backward from the most recent news. By now, he'd been over all of the details and press about the drug bust a hundred times and still couldn't pinpoint who might have set it up.

Taking a long draw on his beer, he pulled up files he'd created on key people in town, especially those who'd vo-calized frustration and concern over the chief's victory speech. The hardware store owner had gone public for a Baltimore news station. The mayor, too, more than once. Riley chalked that up to making the most of free publicity for the hardware store and the mayor was leveraging the attention for his political advancement. The well-spoken politician was nearly as irritating as the whiny Mr. Filmore.

Riley was digging deeper into Filmore's background when the doorbell chimed. He quickly closed the windows related to his search and brought up the remodeling sites that fit his cover story. In the hall, he spied visitors at his kitchen door. Chief Jensen and an older lady. Both were smiling, but only the older woman looked like she was truly happy to be there.

He manufactured a smile and answered the door. "Evening, ladies." He flashed the chief a covert smile.

"Excuse us for dropping in without any warning," the older woman said cheerfully. "I'm Matilda Wilks, just two doors down. Abby here offered to join me in welcoming you to the neighborhood."

Abby's cloudy expression told a much different story. He grinned, knowing she'd either been dragged along or had joined Mrs. Wilks solely for the purpose of checking the Hamiltons' property. His money was on the latter.

"We brought cookies." Mrs. Wilks waved the foil-covered plate in her hand. "Fresh from the oven."

"I'd be a fool to turn you away," Riley said, holding the door wide for them. Let Abby look around. She needed to realize he wasn't a threat to her, even if he couldn't tell her outright that he was her best asset.

Mrs. Wilks bustled in and the scent of warm chocolate-chip cookies tickled his nose. But the scent of Abby, as she strolled past him in the narrow hall, brought his entire body to high alert. She'd let down her hair and the glossy blond mane smelled of flowers warmed by sunshine. While he didn't understand the science behind fragrances, he appreciated the effects.

That scent took him back to the garden behind the orphanage, where he'd first discovered the satisfaction of working with his hands.

"Poor Abby here hadn't heard about the Hamiltons, what with everything she's had on her mind," Mrs. Wilks was saying. Making herself right at home, she put the plate on the table and removed the foil, revealing a pile of thick, perfectly browned chocolate-chip cookies. Then she spotted the beer on the counter. "Tell me you have milk? Or even coffee?"

"Both," he said, grinning.

"Good boy." Mrs. Wilks beamed up at him, her steel-gray hair swinging as she turned to the chief. "Which do you prefer, Abby dear?"

"Milk, please."

Mrs. Wilks arched a brow and gave a soft, speculating hum. "Your stomach must be a bother with all this extra stress."

When a blush crept into the chief's cheeks, Riley tried to distract Mrs. Wilks. "Have a seat," he encouraged, pulling out the nearest chair. Mrs. Wilks claimed the seat. Riley reached for the next chair and smiled at the chief.

"No, thanks," she said, obviously in police chief mode. "Mind if I look around?"

"Abby," Mrs. Wilks scolded, "at least have a cookie before you go investigating."

Riley smothered a laugh while he filled three glasses with milk. "Aside from a suitcase and my laptop, I promise you it's just the way the Hamiltons left it."

"I've told her everything they told me," Mrs. Wilks said. She arrowed Abby a knowing look. "She just doesn't know how to relax."

Abby threw up her hands in surrender and took a seat.

Riley joined them, taking the one remaining chair and being careful not to bump Abby's knee with his.

"A body gets tired of the cold," Mrs. Wilks was saying. "If I had family in Florida, I might do the very same thing."

"I'm not sure I could let you do that," Abby said, choosing a cookie. "Who would bake for me?"

"You know your way around a kitchen, young lady, don't

even pretend. What about you?" She turned a sharp eye his way. "Do you need me to bring over a casserole?"

He grinned at the older woman again. "I can manage. Thanks."

"More than beer and chips, I hope."

"Yes, ma'am." He broke a cookie in two and stuffed one half into his mouth. As he chewed, he watched the way Abby dunked her cookie in her milk glass. Deliberate and methodical, he found it oddly endearing. "The cookies are perfect, Mrs. Wilks. Thanks for bringing them by."

"Good company makes everything better." She looked around the kitchen. "What did the Hamiltons want you to do here?"

"A little of this and that," he replied. "There's some minor repair work I'll take care of first."

"That rotted wood under the sink, I hope. Abby, do you remember what a mess that was?"

Abby bobbed her chin, her mouth full of cookie. Riley smothered a laugh. "I was just debating tile or vinyl. Any thoughts, ladies?"

As Mrs. Wilks launched into a full report of which families on the street had made which type of upgrade, Riley caught the chief watching him.

He arched his eyebrows and her gaze abruptly returned to the glass of milk in front of her. "Another cookie?" He nudged the plate her way.

She shook her head and pushed back from the table.

"You don't have a preference on the flooring?" he asked.

The look she sent him was cool at best. "No. You should go with whatever the owners want," she replied, taking her glass to the sink and rinsing it.

"True," he admitted. "I'll work up a few ideas for them to consider. If it were my place I'd go with tile."

"Hard on the knees," Mrs. Wilks interjected. "Then you just end up with rugs and mats everywhere."

He mentioned the reclaimed hardwood and Mrs. Wilks offered an exuberant opinion on the value of that idea. He pretended not to notice Abby slipping away from the kitchen.

Mrs. Wilks had no such problem. She motioned for him to lean in closer. "That girl is suspicious of everyone these days. Don't let it bother you."

"I hear she has cause."

"That she does," Mrs. Wilks agreed. "Go with the reclaimed floor. Better all around."

"All right," he said, listening to the stair treads creak. He grinned at Mrs. Wilks. "I promise I'm not here to cause more trouble."

"Oh, I could tell that first thing," she said. "She'll relax. Personally, I'm glad to have a strapping young man so close. Makes me feel safe." She got up, put her glass in the sink and walked to the door. "She cooks when she's upset. Based on the groceries she hauled in the other day, there's at least one lasagna in her freezer and another in the oven. You could do worse than get yourself invited to dinner."

Startled by the older woman's suggestion, he didn't have a chance to reply before she was gone. The older woman was a matchmaker. He'd stake his skill with a weapon on it.

He was putting the glasses in the dishwasher when the chief reappeared.

"Where's Mrs. Wilks?"

"Home," he replied, drying his hands. "She said something about dinner in the oven."

"I'm the one with dinner baking," she muttered. She'd been watching his hands with an odd expression, but those blue eyes abruptly locked on to his face.

He looped the towel through the bar on the front of

the dishwasher and tucked his hands into his pockets. She tempted him, her dark, snug jeans hugging her curves and her soft gray cable-knit sweater emphasizing the storms in her eyes. "Are you satisfied now?"

She scowled at him. "With what?"

"Your search," he reminded her. "You were kind of obvious. Whatever you think I am, you're wrong." It was one of the few things he could say with absolute certainty.

"You have no idea what I think about you."

He pushed away from the counter, pleased when she held her ground. Maybe she wasn't seeing him as a threat after all. "Enlighten me," he suggested as he covered the plate of cookies.

"I'm still assessing," she said, reaching for the coat she'd draped over the chair back.

He laughed.

"What's so funny?" She paused, her hands going still on the second toggle of her coat.

"Sorry." He held up his hands. "Just the two of us tiptoeing around the facts."

"Which are?"

"We're neighbors. The whole welcome thing reminds me of something my mom used to say."

"Which is?"

"Not really appropriate." And nonexistent. "Is there anything I could do or say to put you at ease?"

"Tell me what your mom said."

"Maybe another time." He grabbed his beer, taking a long pull from the bottle while he watched her.

"You seem legit," she admitted reluctantly.

"Thanks." He returned the beer to the counter. "I could raise a little hell if it would make you feel better."

"I'd feel better if you stayed at one of the long-term hotels like the rest of the crews."

"Ah. But that's not happening."

"What did your mother say?"

He shook his head. She was tenacious, a trait that must serve her well. "It had to do with snooping and gossip, but it doesn't really apply in this case."

A telltale blush crept into her cheeks. "Why not?"

"Because you were checking the closets for bodies or stolen goods, right?"

"Maybe."

He shrugged. "That's your job," he replied. "And why should I get offended if I'm not hiding anything." Not where she could find it, anyway.

She pursed those full, rose-colored lips, pushing his thoughts into dangerous territory. "Coming over here was Mrs. Wilks's idea."

"I believe you," he said with a smile. "And you made the most of the opportunity. Considering recent events, I would've been more concerned if you hadn't taken a look around."

She pushed back her sleeve and checked her watch. "Still haven't seen the basement," she pointed out.

He gave her a mock grimace. "It's musty and more than a little spooky down there."

"Then you can go first."

"That's a big risk. What'll you give me in return?"

"If we survive, you mean?"

He nodded, liking this playful side of her. "Let's assume the positive."

She checked her watch again. "If we survive, I'll share dinner at my house."

"What's on the menu?"

"What a guy question." She rolled her eyes. "It's lasagna—homemade—and more than enough for two."

"Sounds great. Follow me." He led her into the hallway

and opened the door to the basement. "Don't say I didn't warn you."

"Just move," she said at his back.

He hit the switch and the fluorescent light at the bottom of the stairs slowly brightened.

Riley started down, hearing her footsteps on the wooden stairs echo a half beat after his. Reaching the cement floor, he moved aside so she could examine the space.

She hesitated on the last step, studying him closely while she held a brief height advantage.

Wondering how she saw him, he let her look her fill. It gave him time to return the favor. Her wide blue eyes made him hate the threats that had her wary of everyone around her.

He'd done his homework; he knew what she'd looked like before the drug bust. The new, perpetual scowl was a telltale sign of the damage to her confidence. She'd probably always been cautious, but now she didn't trust anyone. Except maybe Mrs. Wilks.

As she finally moved past him, he caught a whiff of her shampoo again. He cleared his throat. "Storage and laundry to the left—"

"Pinball to the right," she finished for him. "Mr. Hamilton's hobby."

"So you have been down here."

"Not recently." She turned a slow circle. "It's like a time capsule."

It was a valid assessment. "Fortunately they left decent appliances."

"That's a plus." She walked over to the first pinball machine on the short wall.

"Want to play a game or two? It works great."

"No, thanks. I'm obsessive. If I start I won't want to quit and dinner will burn."

"In that case, allow me to see you safely up the stairs."

Her smile chased away the shadows haunting his thoughts. "Thanks for indulging my curiosity."

"My pleasure." He gestured for her to go up first, immediately regretting the chivalry as it put the shapely curve of her hips and backside right at eye level. No one could fault her fitness. Thinking of Director Casey's reaction if such an unprofessional observation showed up in his report cooled him right down.

She didn't seem to pick up on his wayward thoughts, waiting patiently while he locked up and followed her across the driveway and into her kitchen. The houses were similar Cape Cod floor plans, but her decor reflected a more modern sense of style. He liked it.

"How are the knees?" He pointed to the large ceramic tiles under her feet.

"Just fine," she replied as the oven timer went off.

So much for asking for a tour of her place.

"My biggest adjustment was the cold," she said, pulling the large pan out of the oven.

"I didn't think of that."

"No one does. Go for the reclaimed hardwood."

He nodded in agreement. The remodeling ideas were coming to him almost as quickly as questions regarding the drug bust. But he hesitated to wreck the momentum by quizzing her about that case. "Man, that smells good."

"It tastes better."

She put him to work tossing a salad while she pulled the lasagna out of the oven, letting it stand while she set the table.

He hadn't been hungry until he'd walked in. The rich aroma of sausage, cheese, tomato sauce and oregano had his mouth watering in anticipation by the time she served.

"Whoa," he said, setting down his fork after the first bite. "That's amazing."

"Thanks. It's the sauce."

"Here I thought it was the company."

She rolled her eyes. "Do you always come on so strong?"

He shrugged, taking another bite and giving himself time to think of a reasonable reply. "Call me a doer," he said, keeping it light. "All my life I've seen people waste time and effort waffling about what they want and how to get it."

"Are you saying you want me?" Her eyebrows arched, silently daring him to reply honestly.

He grinned at her. "I'm saying I decided to live my life differently. Focused on the moment."

"Interesting philosophy."

"It's working so far." They ate in silence for a few minutes more. "Looking at you, Madam Police Chief, I'd say that's pretty close to your philosophy, too."

She raised her water glass in a toast. "Close enough." She sipped, returned the glass to the table. "And my friends call me Abby."

"I've moved up from suspicious stranger to friend?"

She chuckled. "It's a long ladder, but you're on your way. You were nice to Mrs. Wilks."

"That's easy."

"Remember that when she starts asking the personal questions."

"I'm an open book."

She snorted. "I think Danny is infatuated with you, but he's a fair judge of character."

"Danny's impressionable," Riley said with a laugh. "He'll be a good neighborhood cop one day."

"He needs experience. Have you remodeled many old homes?"

He recognized a diversionary topic when he heard one,

but if it kept her at ease, kept him close enough to protect her, it worked for him. "A few. I've been swinging a hammer since I was about eight."

"A calling?"

He thought about those early days in the orphanage garden. "I guess so. A completed job, done well, is a reward in itself," he replied, echoing the teachers who'd raised him.

"Another phrase from your mother?"

He nodded, letting her make the assumptions that supported his cover story. "Do you need help with anything around here?"

"Not today."

"Say the word if you change your mind. What about your calling? Have you always been interested in criminal justice?"

"My uncle was a cop and I thought he was the coolest thing going," she said. "Whenever I got the chance, I'd go down to the station and hang out. Talk about impressionable."

"Doesn't sound like a place for a kid."

"My parents worried, but I've always thought it depends on the kid."

"There's some truth to that," he agreed. "Are you thinking kids trashed the sign?"

"I'd like it to be."

"Meaning?" He leaned back in his chair, debating another serving. He was full, but he wanted to keep her talking. Danny had given him some insight about the community, but Abby would have a better overall picture.

"I've been thinking kids wouldn't have been so careful."

"I'm not following. It looked like a fast and dirty tag to me."

"I think it was supposed to look that way," she agreed.

"But how many kids, moving fast enough to not be seen by traffic, would think to cover their footprints?"

"You're sure they didn't just get lucky?"

"I'm sure the tracks were deliberately concealed." She blotted her lips and set the napkin next to her plate. "I need to think about something else. More lasagna?"

"Twist my arm," he said, reaching for the pan. "What's the secret with the sauce?"

"If I told you, it wouldn't be a secret."

"Tell me anyway. You'll feel better."

"I feel fine now."

"But there's so much more to life than 'fine,'" he teased with a wink.

She opened her mouth but whatever she'd been about to say was cut off by a loud crash outside. They were both on their feet in an instant. He followed her as she raced through the house and out the front door.

Across the street, a man was caught under an extension ladder, a reel of brightly colored Christmas lights still blinking in his hand. Riley swore, reaching for his cell phone to dial 911 while Abby kept running. Mrs. Wilks and others were soon in the street, wondering how to help and speculating on what happened.

ABBY TOLD HERSELF this was only an accident as she ran across the street. Letting her instincts take over, she shouted for blankets and they appeared moments later.

"An ambulance is on the way," Riley said, appearing beside her. "Hang in there," he said to the man under the ladder.

"Well, this is a fine way to meet your neighbors," Abby said briskly. "Riley O'Brien, this is Roy Calder."

"Everyone calls me Calder. Wish I could say it was a pleasure," he added through gritted teeth.

"Does it hurt everywhere?" Riley took the lights out of Calder's grip.

"Yeah."

"Good."

"Riley!" Abby pushed him back. "What are you doing?"

"He's right," Calder said. "Feeling everything means my back's in one piece."

"Oh." She hadn't thought of the injuries in terms of potential paralysis. "That is good." Abby rubbed the chill from her arms, accepting a coat that appeared from somewhere. Mrs. Wilks was cheerfully scolding their neighbor for working without a net.

"I was almost done," he defended. "Anyone see the bastard who pushed the ladder?"

Abby shivered with a chill that had nothing to do with the cold. "What did you say, Calder?"

"I'm not an idiot, Chief, despite the looks of this. Someone brought me down on purpose."

She looked around the scene wondering who might have done such a terrible thing. All she saw were the familiar faces of her neighbors looking as stunned as she felt. "Did you get a look?"

"No more than a glimpse of a dark knit cap when I felt something at the ladder."

"Back everyone up," she said to Riley, hoping he could manage crowd control. She wished she'd remembered to grab her phone. She was going to need someone to help her walk the area and look for evidence. But first things first. She knelt beside Calder again. "What did you hear?"

Calder groaned a little, either thinking about it or just struggling to breathe. "A crunch. Boots on the landscaping."

"Okay. Good." Calder's wife used white rock in the flower beds. Covered in snow, the assailant must have miscalculated. "What else? A car? A bike?"

"No. That's about it. I was falling before I could even shout at him to stop."

She looked at Calder's house. "Did he come from your left or right?"

"The left." Calder groaned again. "Christ. Libby will kill me. I wanted to get this done for her tonight."

"Maybe I should question her," Abby said, teasing him. Libby was known as one of the gentlest people in Belclare. And she was seven months pregnant with their second child.

Calder's laughter turned into a cough. "I'm sure she feels she has cause to do me harm more days than not."

Abby pasted a smile on her face as the paramedics arrived and took over. As she backed out of the way, she hit an immovable wall. Before she could apologize, she felt warm hands on her shoulders, steadying her. "Easy. I've got you."

Riley. His touch was somehow calming. But that didn't last long. Anger, shock and worry spun like a wild tornado in her belly as Calder was moved first to the backboard and then to the ambulance.

When the ambulance was gone, Abby walked toward the landscaping to have a look.

"You should go inside," Riley said from right behind her.

"No." She faced him. This close, she had to tip her head back to meet his gaze. "He thinks someone pushed the ladder. I need to call in some help and check out the scene."

His eyes narrowed and his mouth, usually so quick with that wry grin, turned into a dark frown. He handed her his phone. "Make the call. I'll clear out the spectators."

He managed the task efficiently and politely, turning down offers to help clean up the mess while she explained the situation to the officer on duty at the station.

When Riley returned, the street was eerily quiet.

"Here." He handed her a heavy flashlight. "Figured you'd need that."

"Thanks." She wasn't sure what she hoped to find, but it wasn't the nasty note scrawled on the siding of Calder's house: "One down. Who's next?"

"Not paint. Looks like charcoal," Riley observed.

"Guess Calder was right about being pushed." *Open season on Belclare.* The media would be showing that all night long and as soon as the word got around about this, the rest of the town would know Calder was in the hospital because of her.

Her stomach clutched and she nearly tossed her dinner right there at the scene. Anger jolted her. She'd never come close to contaminating a crime scene in her career. "Damn it. If they want me, they should come at *me*."

"They want you to suffer."

Knowing he was right made her feel worse. "What am I supposed to do, leave town? How would that help anyone?"

"That might be the most important question."

She glared at him, wishing the light was better. "You sound more like a cop than a carpenter."

"From you, I'll take that as a compliment."

"It wasn't meant that way."

"Too bad. I'd think you know from experience that very few people do bad things for the fun of it." He flashed the light on the grim message again. "It's kind of obvious someone is trying to get under your skin."

To her ultimate frustration, it was working.

She didn't know what to make of her new neighbor. He had a presence people responded to, herself included. His easygoing manners didn't quite fit with his critical thinking. And how insensitive of her to think a guy with a tool belt had only one dimension.

She had enough experience with people to know better,

but something about Riley was different. Something more than the way her body went hot when he was close. Whatever else she felt, this was hardly the time to address her physical attraction to him.

"Do you see any footprints?" The beam from the flashlight sliced through the darkness as she searched for anything helpful.

"Too many," he answered.

That new urge to scream returned with a vengeance. She wouldn't give the people behind these hateful acts the satisfaction. Whatever system she'd disrupted with the drug bust, the criminals were playing hardball now. She'd read the emails and threats in chat rooms about retaliation that involved taking out innocent civilians. Until now, she'd thought it was so much smoke and hot air.

They were lucky Calder hadn't been paralyzed or even killed.

When she found the person responsible—and she silently vowed to do just that—she would see them rot behind bars.

When an investigative team arrived, Abby relinquished the scene as soon as she brought them up to speed. With her head spinning, she would only impede their progress. Belclare deserved the best from their police department.

Trudging back across the street, she could almost hear the gossip chasing her. The graffiti on the welcome sign was bad enough. As word spread about Calder she'd be lucky if Mayor Scott didn't fire her at the next town council meeting.

He didn't exactly have the authority, but that wouldn't stop the posturing. And the posturing would weaken her position. Reaching her front door, she glanced back over her shoulder one last time, but the view of Calder's house was blocked by Riley's wide shoulders. "What are you doing?"

"Relax." He rubbed a hand gently across her shoulder,

making her want to lean in for a hug. "I was going to help you clean up the kitchen."

"No, thanks. You've done more than enough to help me tonight." This time she *was* praising him and he shuffled his feet, apparently uncomfortable with the compliment. Interesting.

"Let's try again tomorrow." He signaled to the Hamiltons' house. "At my place."

She sighed. Being around her wasn't smart. The vandals and Calder's attacker proved that. "I can't tell if you're brave or a glutton for punishment."

"A guy could say the same about you," he replied with a grin.

No. Most men said different things about her. Aside from Deke, Riley was the first man who seemed to see beyond her title and badge. She caught the flash of cameras across the street and hoped her detectives were coming up with something useful.

"Tomorrow night I have plans." If she had the courage to explore a new path in her relationship with Deke. She'd been looking forward to the potential with the artist. Now, with a new neighbor bent on hovering, it seemed she might have a choice. Did she want one?

Right now she wanted some quiet. "Thanks for your help, Riley."

He nodded, gracing her with a slow smile she found so much more attractive than his grin. "Be sure to lock your doors."

"I think that's my line."

"Not tonight, Abby. I'm right next door if you need me."

Baffled by the temptation he presented, she escaped into her house, throwing the dead bolt and security chain. She didn't need to look to know he'd waited to be sure she locked up.

In the kitchen, she checked the lock on the back door and pulled the curtains. As she cleaned up dinner, her thoughts wandered between Deke and Riley and she told herself it was an exercise in distraction. It would be years before that horrible image of Calder under the ladder faded from her memory.

Ruthlessly, she forced her mind to lighter issues. As much as she enjoyed Deke, Riley stirred some new, previously undefined feminine flutter. Her girlfriends would blame it on the tool belt, and they might have a point. He had good hands, too, broad and strong.

And warm, she remembered, thinking of how he'd touched her when the ambulance arrived.

She was smart enough to know better, wise enough to look past the handsome face and sexy features to the man underneath. Yet she entertained a purely physical fantasy as she headed upstairs to bed.

What in the world was going on with her? The man was a stranger....

And, with an unknown enemy haunting her, a stranger was the last thing she needed in her life right now.

Chapter Six

"Sir, a call."

Deke set aside his novel. The sitting room where he chatted weekly with Abby had become his favorite place to plan and strategize. He watched the fire in the hearth, waiting until his assistant had pulled the door closed before dealing with the caller, "Yes?"

"I went by, but she had company."

"Explain," Deke replied. The news startled him at first. Abby never had company. He knew her habits as well as his own.

"I drove by with the channel open and I heard voices."

This was no cause for alarm. Her company was likely just a brief visit with her neighbor. The older woman played mother to the entire block. She would have heard about the vandalism and come by to offer moral support.

It couldn't be allowed to continue. Deke needed Abby to come to him. He'd been waiting for hours for her to show up and cry on his shoulder—or in the manner more suitable to Abby—ask his advice. With the fear he'd incited among the citizens of her beloved town, he'd made himself her only friend in this dumpy, godforsaken place and his patience was growing thin.

"I waited and then came in closer," his employee continued. "Looks like the guy from one of those setup teams.

The one who's been working at the department. They looked pretty cozy."

The guy? Cozy? Deke's hand clutched the upholstered arm of his chair. That couldn't be possible. She wouldn't take the risk. He'd thoughtfully and carefully nurtured her paranoia to the point that she didn't trust anyone.

"Find out who he is. I want everything you can find on him."

"I'm on it."

What could she be thinking? The idea of his trophy, his *reward,* spending her time with one of the temporary workers passing through town, set his temper blazing. He didn't fight it, letting it burn, vaporizing the haze of his misplaced esteem and affection for Abigail Jensen. She was now his enemy with no potential for redemption.

"Updates every hour. I want pictures, as well."

"Already handled."

"Really?" Deke knew better than to ask how. It was satisfying to have something going right. The people he hired quickly learned about his zero tolerance for failure. He supposed he owed the man some encouragement. "This afternoon's vandalism was good work."

"Thank you."

"You can trust them to keep quiet?" Deke wondered about the misfits the man had hired to deface the town's historic welcome sign.

"I don't trust anyone that much."

"Good." It was the tacit confirmation he wanted that the vandals were dead. Dead men didn't tell tales. "I'll leave you to it."

The call ended and Deke walked to the window that overlooked the water. It was a worthy view of the quaint little town when the moon was full. Tonight it was dull and gray, the sky full of clouds. Mother Nature seemed all too willing to accommodate Belclare's hope for a fresh blanket of picturesque snow to kick off their annual event.

The only good thing about the tourist season was the potential for more victims and even more suspects. The police department would have no rest until the next shipment was safely through. And when he was done with Abigail Jensen, when she was thoroughly ruined and dead at his feet, Deke promised himself he would move from this insipid place. He wanted to find somewhere with more space and more sunshine to go with his anonymity.

With his endgame in mind, he called in his assistant and gave the next orders. Yes, a fresh blanket of snow would fit perfectly into his plan. That way the spilled blood would show up a vivid red.

Chapter Seven

Abby rushed through the back door toward her office, already an hour behind schedule and her mind a jumble of details that needed to be handled swiftly. Checking on her neighbor this morning had taken longer than she'd expected, but it had been necessary. Calder was a friend, and now, a victim. Learning who might have wanted to hurt him to get to her was essential.

Then she'd discovered someone had broken into her garage last night. Nothing appeared to be missing or damaged—except her pride, which was exactly why she had no intention of making a formal report on it. If the chief of police couldn't protect her own home, how was she going to protect the town? She shook her head. The feds would holler again about protection and security. Maybe they had a point. The extra patrols would have to be enough—the people she was responsible for in this community took priority. With any luck they'd catch the troublemaker before a security system could be installed. Maybe she was losing it? Her mind and her ability to get the job done.

No time to debate the latter. This morning's delays had cost her valuable mental prep time going into today's meeting with Mayor Scott and Martin Filmore. Sadly, she couldn't put off this potential minefield. Both men were waiting for her and came to their feet as she walked in. Their easy presence in her office made her want to shoot something.

"Good morning," she offered, not even trying to smile.

"You're fifteen minutes late," Mayor Scott said.

"I hope the sergeant made you comfortable." Based on the two cups of coffee on her desk, it looked as if they were comfortable enough.

She put her coat on the rack and set her purse to the side before taking her seat.

"Have you found the vandals?"

She'd had the entire twenty seconds of walking across the police station to read that report. "Not yet. The team posted last night didn't encounter any more trouble." She shifted her full attention to Martin. "Have you come up with plan of action for restoring the welcome sign?"

"I met with the decorating company, yes. They agreed to create a temporary sign while the original is removed and sent for restoration."

Mayor Scott cleared his throat. "The town council released the appropriate funds."

"That is good news," Abby said. "My officers have reorganized their schedules and patrol routes to—"

"Is that absolutely necessary?" Martin interrupted.

"Yes, Mr. Filmore," Abby replied, struggling for control. "As I explained yesterday, based on recent events, I believe the extra patrols are imperative to keeping this city safe. In fact, I was about to ask—" she glanced at the mayor "—for a small slice of the emergency funds to hire a few extra officers from Baltimore for the opening weekend."

"No."

She blinked at the mayor's stern response. "Excuse me?"

"We've had enough public attention of the wrong kind. The media has painted a target on Belclare. We'll be lucky if we aren't facing a ghost town this weekend. Are you trying to bankrupt our city, Chief?"

Abby clamped her mouth shut, startled by this one-hundred-eighty degree turnaround from the man who didn't believe in the concept of bad publicity. How had everything and everyone around her changed so suddenly? The answer followed hot on the heels of that question. *Fear.* The kind of fear her actions had brought to the citizens of Belclare changed people.

Nothing she could do about that. Protecting the citizens was her job. Appeasing them—if it got in the way—was not.

"I concur," Mr. Filmore added with an arrogant tilt of his chin.

Of course he concurred. These guys were the drama twins, each with a slightly differing agenda. She laced her fingers together, wishing for her own cup of coffee, but that would have to wait. "The town council will approve the overtime expenses for my officers." It wasn't a question. Fortunately for the mayor, he seemed to understand that, as well. A vague dip of his head showed acknowledgment even if he would never say as much out loud. She moved on. "My officers are not on patrol to threaten or interfere with anyone, but in our experience a vigilant, visible presence is its own deterrent."

"It didn't deter more trouble on your street last night," Filmore blurted out, his face turning red with frustration. "You all but sent out engraved invitations for every criminal to come test you. Belclare will pay the ultimate price."

She bit back the sharp retort dancing on the tip of her tongue. "What would you have me do differently, Mr. Filmore?"

His mouth flapped like a fish for several seconds. "I'm not qualified to say, but I have gumption enough to know what you've done so far isn't working." He turned to the mayor. "All I know is that what you're doing is ruining the most important time of year for our town."

Gutless wonders, both of them, she thought. Their support for her success with the drug bust had shifted with the arrival of the very first federal agent. The instant the first threat hit the airwaves she was public enemy number one with these two men.

"Well, I must admit the generous promotional spots Deke Maynard provided should go a long way to salvaging opening weekend," Mayor Scott allowed, smoothing a hand over his glaring holiday-plaid tie.

Ghost town or a decent turnout? She wished he'd pick a theory and stick with it.

On the short drive into the office, she'd only caught a teaser about Deke's upcoming call-in interview on the radio. The man rarely bothered with publicity and she knew it made him uncomfortable, but if he was in her corner, urging people to attend the Christmas Village, she owed him a big thank-you.

"Will you at least decorate the police cars?" the historic society's president asked.

"That's a favorite tradition around here, Mr. Filmore," Abby agreed. "I'll make sure someone takes care of that right away." She'd already assigned Danny to follow up on that detail, but she didn't see the need to let Filmore know she'd had the idea first. Maybe appeasing was necessary at this point.

"Thank you," he allowed.

Never an easy person to be around, Filmore fidgeted more than usual today. She chalked it up to distress over the ruination of the heirloom welcome sign on top of his disapproval of her new patrol protocol.

Both men stood. Finally. With handshakes and an exchange of "Merry Christmas," they left her alone in her office.

Turning to her computer, she found websites for the local television and radio stations. The impromptu media junket Deke had managed this morning was getting an outpouring of positive responses. The man had single-handedly muted the negative press regarding the crime wave in Belclare. Offering an additional painting for the silent auction that benefitted the Belclare Food Bank was a lure that would bring in serious tourist traffic. Maynard rarely sold his original paintings, though he displayed new work in the local gallery and occasionally chose pieces for limited commercial print runs. Abby was overwhelmed with gratitude for the man who seemed to be her only ally in town. She picked up her cell phone and dialed his number.

His assistant answered in his typical muted monotone and, moments later, Deke's voice filled her ear.

"Darling, how are you today?"

Better than Calder, she thought with no small measure of guilt. While the officers who'd taken over the search had found tracks in the snow behind the house, they'd lost the trail at the next street. "At the moment I'm out of the mayor's doghouse," she replied. "Thanks to you."

"Anything for a friend. We can't let something as silly and petty as vandals get in the way of a good tourist season."

She wished petty and silly crimes were all she had to think about. "Well, once more you've put your support into action and I'm immensely grateful."

"Does that mean you'll skip your meeting and join me this evening?"

She hesitated. Was that what she wanted it to mean? Sharing dinner with Deke would be a marvelous escape from a typical evening. She indulged in the fantasy, imagining the balm of excellent food paired with the perfect wine and intelligent conversation in front of the fireplace in his dining room. Would anything be better?

An image of those threats on the welcome sign and then on her neighbor's house blotted out her fantasy. She tried to shake it off, but the memory of Calder pinned under the ladder shivered through her.

"Abby? Are you there?"

"Yes, of course." Her palms went clammy. Calder was a good neighbor. He'd made minor repairs around her house, sometimes in exchange for only a six-pack of beer. It helped to have a neighbor like him when she didn't have time for a man in her life otherwise. Was time really the problem or was it just another excuse? She pushed the thought away and answered Deke's question. "Yes. Sorry, I'm here. As much as I'd like to join you, I'm afraid I will have to pass on dinner."

She pressed her thumb to the point between her eyebrows, hoping to ease another wave of tension. Putting off Deke after he'd done so much for her felt like an insult. At the very least it felt like she was taking him for granted. She didn't want to visit him in the hospital, either. Someone out there had made a public vow to hurt her and the people she cared about. The threats weren't going away and the problem was escalating. Whoever put the vandals and assailants in motion knew how to get under her skin. Injuring her neighbor and going through her garage were way too close for comfort. She didn't dare consider what might be next.

"Are you sure?" he pressed.

She'd offended him. "I value you, Deke," she confessed,

hoping he'd understand. "As a citizen and as a friend. Whoever wants me out of here is willing to hurt those around me to make a point. I don't want them to hurt you."

"I'm quite capable of watching out for myself," he assured her.

The tension in his voice had given way to something gentler. She could picture that barely there smile on his face. "You've done a fine job." Abby rocked back in her chair. "Will you give me a rain check on dinner?"

He sighed. "Tonight, tomorrow, next week. Whatever best suits your crime-fighting schedule. Consider the invitation open."

"Thank you. That means a great deal." And when this was behind her, she'd make up for lost time.

"Is that just the chief of police talking?"

"No." Was he flirting with her? "True friends seem hard to find under the current circumstances."

"I'm here for you, Abby."

She felt her cheeks heat with his steady reassurance. Thank goodness, they weren't having this talk in person. What was it about this man that made her waffle so much? One minute she wanted him to be more than a friend, the next she wasn't so sure. "I'll be in touch, Deke. Thank you again for going above and beyond for opening weekend. Please be careful and call in if you need any assistance."

"Always. You do the same."

"Definitely." She was smiling when the call disconnected and it felt genuine for the first time in ages. This nonsense in the media and with whomever had decided to terrify her town had only started a little over a week ago, but she couldn't deny the stress was taking a toll.

She checked the time. It was too soon to expect any news from the officers who'd come by when she'd found her garage door hanging open. With little more than half an hour before the hardware store opened for business, she decided to check her email. Buying a new lock for the garage wouldn't be a high point of her day, but she needed it secure for her peace of mind. And a new snow shovel to deal with the fresh snow predicted for this evening. Hers had been taken to the crime lab to analyze what had appeared to be dried blood on the blade. The idea that someone had *borrowed* her snow shovel and used it for something untoward was a little out there, as theories went, but considering the other strange happenings around here lately she wasn't taking any chances.

Half an hour would be enough time to review the overflowing email in-box and send any threat with a clear target up the line to the feds.

Braced for more hateful messages, she set to work.

RILEY TURNED DOWN the volume on the radio clipped to his ladder. All of Belclare was enamored with Deke Maynard and his unflinching support of Chief Jensen. It was the third time this morning he'd heard the new ad for the Christmas Village opening weekend.

The artist—in his mind he added a sneer to the word— made him edgy. There was more going on behind the sparkling windows of the man's perfectly restored home. A great deal more than the sketches and scenic oils on canvas displayed with such care in the gallery window down the street evoked.

Riley knew his role here. He understood that he couldn't jump at every shadow while he was learning the landscape. This wasn't a short game Casey had him playing.

That didn't necessarily rule out the immediate trouble closing in on Chief Jensen. Filmore, the uptight snob who wanted to lift the added patrols, particularly the foot patrols, was near the top of Riley's list. The man's priorities were way off. Being passionate about architecture and history was fine. But what kind of person preferred historical accuracy over the safety of the general public?

A man with something to hide, in Riley's opinion. Or something more to gain.

In less than two days, the Christmas Village would be hosting the first major rush of tourists for the season. So far, he hadn't pinpointed a clear threat, but someone was ramping up the effort against the chief.

According to Danny, Chief Jensen was spending an inordinate amount of time behind closed doors since the drug bust, sorting out the loonies from the more substantial threats that were flooding the station's snail mail and email every day. Chief Jensen sent high-level threats to the feds for further analysis. Anything Director Casey could tie to Belclare, he sent back to Riley, but so far, no hard intel had come his way.

He'd overheard people whispering about the vandalism and the attack on Calder; however, there weren't any leads beyond wild speculation and fingers pointing at him and the other temporary workers in town. The easy theory wasn't close to accurate when it came to him and he didn't suspect any of his co-workers. But in a community as close as Belclare it was far more comfortable and convenient to blame outsiders.

Whoever was behind the trouble was using human nature to their advantage. Surely a cop as smart as Jensen wouldn't have settled for that lousy, easy explanation. But Riley wondered why the person or group behind all this thought she would.

He took his assignment for the day—the hardware store on Main Street—and knocked it out in record time with the help of two other guys from the crew.

While they tested lights and put the final touches on

the displays, Riley casually observed the people watching them. There was decent foot traffic in the business center of town and for the most part people were cautiously friendly. He might have a lifetime assignment here, but it wouldn't be a hardship. It wasn't as if he had family or a significant other waiting somewhere else. He could see a place like this being home.

With a few minutes before the next load of decorations from the warehouse was due, he walked into the hardware store to look around. An agent's best asset was a thorough knowledge of the situation.

"Welcome, welcome," an older woman behind the counter greeted him. "You look like a man who needs a new pair of gloves."

He pulled his cold, red hands from the pockets of his vest and blew on them a little. "I don't use gloves with close work like this."

"Well, that's understandable," she allowed. "Take your time and warm up some anyway."

"That wind can be a bear," he said, hoping he sounded friendly. He wanted to get her talking. Listening to the chatter among the locals was another excellent tool for assignments like this one.

"Part of the charm this close to the water," she replied with a twinkle in her bright blue eyes. "Only the tough ones stick it out. Will you be moving on soon?"

He hesitated at the aisle with bins of nails and fasteners stretched out on either side. "I might be around a while." He shot her a grin. "I'll get used to the charm. And I already have another job lined up in Belclare when the decorations are done."

"That's good news, I suppose."

Riley recognized the curiosity in her voice. She was

interested in his wallet as well as his purpose. He'd happily use that lead-in. "I think so."

"That company you're working for knows your plans?"

He stepped up to the counter, ready to play the gossip game. "They know I earn every penny of what they pay me and that's enough."

"Hmm."

He stuck out his hand. "Riley O'Brien," he said. "Do you handle special orders?"

The older woman's eyes lit up. "Of course. Peg Blackwell, at your service."

"Pleased to meet you, Ms. Blackwell."

"Peg."

Riley acknowledged the correction with a quick nod. "I find myself in need of—"

The bell over the door jingled, interrupting the request he'd been about to make. He found himself in need, but the context changed at the sight of Chief Jensen. He glanced at Peg, wondering if she'd hit a silent alarm to summon the chief when he'd walked in. Did he look that suspicious?

"Good morning, Peg," Abby called, wiping her feet on the doormat.

"Chief," the lady behind the counter replied.

Riley surveyed his assignment. The chief looked overdressed for a hardware store, in a soft Christmas-red sweater and charcoal slacks with heeled boots far too dressy for the weather. Her cheeks were bright pink from the cold and a wisp of blond hair had escaped from her ponytail and caught in her lip gloss.

He struggled to ignore the feelings she roused in him. Yes, he'd been sent to protect her, but he was taking her safety much too personally—in record time at that.

Behind the counter, Peg's demeanor shifted and she gave off a vibe as cold as the biting wind outside. No love lost between these two, Riley decided, wondering if it was just the recent trouble or if their problems went deeper. Not everyone in town was a potential terrorist, but someone was the ringleader of all the trouble falling on Belclare and the police chief.

"Good morning, Mr. O'Brien."

He corrected her with a slow shake of his head.

She sighed and tucked a wayward lock of hair behind her ear. "Good morning, Riley. Is that your work out front?"

"It sure is," Peg volunteered.

"I had some help along the way," he said.

"It looks good." Abby gifted him with a smile.

"Thanks." He gave her a small bow. "I was about to look over some wood stain options while I wait for the next decorating assignment."

"Aisle three, near the corner," Peg suggested warmly. Her tone dropped several degrees when she spoke to the chief. "What brings you by?"

Riley ambled away, visions in his head of the options for the kitchen while he eavesdropped on the women at the counter.

"I need a new lock set for my garage," Abby said. "And a snow shovel."

Questions rattled through Riley's head and he hoped Peg would ask them. He hadn't spotted any problems at her place before he'd driven in to work.

"Was it frozen?" Peg asked. "You could've asked Calder to have a look. That is, if he wasn't in the hospital."

Ah, so that was the crux of it. Peg and Calder were friends and the lady was blaming the chief for his injury. Wasn't fair. Abby hadn't scrawled that threat on the guy's house and she hadn't pushed over the ladder. None of this was her fault. Whether these people wanted to face it or not, trouble was brewing in their idyllic little town. The only thing Abby was guilty of was drawing it to the surface.

"Not frozen. Just broken. I guess it wasn't as sturdy as it should have been."

He admired Abby's patience with the constant doubt and irritation. Compared to the threats he knew she was receiving, a little grumpiness must feel like a cakewalk. Riley listened as Peg led Abby to the correct aisle for locks.

"Front of the store for the shovel," Peg explained, sounding friendlier in Riley's opinion. "They're calling for a couple of inches tomorrow night."

He couldn't hear Abby's answer as the women walked farther from him, but Peg came to his rescue with a startled explanation that carried through the store.

"Good grief. Are you okay?"

Abby must have answered in the affirmative because suddenly Peg's tone changed again. "I respect what it takes to do your job, young lady, but your mouth has put us all in a world of hurt."

Riley started across the store, ready to leap to Abby's defense. He couldn't be the only person in Belclare who recognized her decisions were rooted in her unflagging dedication.

"What happened?" he demanded, ignoring the way Abby jumped at his interruption. "Did the crime-scene techs find something at Calder's place?"

"No." Abby cleared her throat. "Someone broke the lock on my garage. It's nothing to worry about."

"I don't think so," Riley challenged. "You live right next door to me. If there's some twisted prowler in our neighborhood, I'd like to know how to help you catch him."

Peg's jaw dropped, her expression shifting from disapproval to shock. *Good.* The citizens of Belclare should realize Abby Jensen was doing her job and doing it well. At great personal risk. She might have tossed out an ultimatum in the heat of victory over the drug bust, but he couldn't be the only person around here capable of seeing how she was backing it up. Or trying to.

The email brief he'd read this morning detailed chatter about another drug shipment heading this way. It would likely come through the docks, but there were plenty of vendors descending on the town, as well. In short, the suspect pool was growing instead of shrinking. The situation was overwhelming for a department as small as Abby's.

"I can do it," Abby said.

"That's obvious," Riley agreed, "but we can all use a little help sometimes." She frowned at him so he barreled on with a subject change. "Looks like you're dressed for another press conference. I'll get the lock fixed while you deal with whatever is already on your schedule."

Her frown deepened to a scowl. "What do you know about how I dress?"

"YouTube is everywhere," he said, shooting her a grin. "I keep up with local events. And I heard the ads that artist guy in town put out this morning."

"Deke Maynard?" Her frustration turned to confusion. "What about him?"

"That's the one." He held out his hand. "You'll back up his good publicity with another statement, right?"

She nodded. "Sure. Of course."

"Thought so. Since you have your hands full keeping the peace and chasing the bad guys, give me the lock." When she dropped it into his hand he barely stifled a cheer. "Now, what happened to your snow shovel?"

"We bagged it and sent it to the lab. I don't know that there's anything to officially report as of yet." She shrugged. "For that matter, the material on the blade may not have been blood, but I'll feel better when I've confirmed one way or the other. I'm optimistic since we haven't heard about any victims lying around."

"Give it time," Peg muttered under her breath as she headed back toward the sales counter. "Will that be cash or charge?"

"Cash," Abby said, following her. "Thanks for your help, Peg."

"Anytime." The older woman's demeanor had softened a bit more.

"You're sure you have time for this, Riley?" Abby asked him.

He nodded, hearing the distinct groan of the brakes on the truck he was expecting from the warehouse. "I'll take care of it as soon as I get home."

"The department is running an extra patrol around our street," Abby warned. "Be prepared to let them know you're helping me out."

"Sure thing."

She paid for her purchases, but he carried them out to his truck after she left. Knowing she hadn't assaulted any-one, he wondered who wanted her out of the way so badly they'd resort to planting evidence in her garage. And why hadn't she wanted to file an official report about it?

The bigger question remained: What else could he do to stay close enough to protect her?

Chapter Eight

Frustrated after her security meeting with the Christmas Village vendors, Abby drove home, the hard-rock music pumped as high as she dared. Just as she'd been walking out of her office, the crime lab had called. They identified the tissue on the blade of her snow shovel as human, but it was too early to have any results back on DNA that might match up with evidence in the various databases. The relevant concern was the traces of spray paint in the hair fibers.

She'd vowed to keep this town safe no matter the cost. It wouldn't take much media speculation to convince people she'd taken justice into her own hands. She would never kill someone over graffiti, but just the rumor of it could ruin her career. There was no way to keep the incident off the record now. In fact, her hasty decision could work against her.

God, she was tired.

Gadsden had taken her report, but they both knew being at home in bed alone wasn't enough of an alibi even for a police chief. She'd earned a bit of sympathy and leeway because of the threats raining down on her head, but at some point last night or early this morning, someone with evil intent had been close enough to break in and plant evidence on her snow shovel. Damn it, this was exactly why she needed a dog. But what dog wanted a home with a human who was rarely there?

Her emotions had run the gamut from shock to vengeance as she'd waded through the rest of her crappy day. Someone was screwing with her and she vowed to get to the bottom of it.

Her press conference had gone well, thanks to the unexpected personal appearance of their resident celebrity. Deke hadn't said anything, but he certainly was going out of his way to help her weather the storm. She appreciated that, but siding with her so publicly put him right in the line of fire. As much as she appreciated his support, she worried he would regret giving it. On some level, she understood this was his way of showing he cared. She suspected he didn't do that often. Whether that made her special or not, she wasn't clear on just yet. Her and Deke's relationship—friendship, whatever it was—was complicated.

The worst part was that other than a few reporters she didn't recognize, most of the folks who'd showed up to watch the press conference in person were lifelong residents of Belclare.

In the days following the drug bust, she found herself looking twice at people she'd known for years. Wondering what was going on behind closed doors—or worse—closed minds. It didn't help that she saw the same dark curiosity in the community as people looked at each other. And at her.

It seemed common sense and yet support was too much to ask for these days. Even Peg had been nearly hostile about the recent problems and potential economic fallout. The department received more calls every day from concerned citizens sure the various outsiders helping with the Christmas Village were causing the trouble. Soothing those worries was only dragging down morale at the station, but she didn't know how to turn things around.

Abby had to admit, in the quiet of her car, that she wasn't very accepting of the few people who were offering sup-

port to her and her department. It seemed business owners like Peg were siding with Mayor Scott's opinion that
she'd gone too far and put everyone's livelihood in jeopardy. Deke had probably saved opening weekend, but that
didn't get her off the hook. The mayor clearly wanted her
to do more to smooth the ruffled feathers.

At the light, she debated driving up and thanking Deke
personally. But knowing how much he valued his privacy,
she headed home instead. No sense alienating him, too,
just because she wanted a shoulder to lean on. And though
he'd invited her to dinner once more when the media had
dispersed, he'd done enough for her today.

Thoughts of Deke's shoulder slipped right out of her
mind as she turned onto her street. Her neighbors had been
busy while she'd been sorting through threats, suspects
and a frightening lack of witnesses. Christmas lights outlined roofs and shrubs; lawn ornaments featuring scenes
from reindeer pulling sleighs to gentle nativities glowed
on snow-dusted lawns.

But the gas lamp posts in each yard... Wow! Who had
managed to get all of the neighbors to do that? Parking in
her driveway, she got out of her car and admired the effect
of wide red and white ribbons that turned each lamp post
into a candy cane. Even hers. Happiness washed over her
that whoever had come up with the idea had automatically
included her. The effect was unifying yet neutral enough
that it didn't fight with the individual displays each family preferred. Belatedly, she noticed that even the tall generic streetlights at each end of the block were similarly
decorated.

With the heart of Belclare becoming a Christmas Village each year, the residential areas joined in, too. It was a
friendly competition within each neighborhood. Exhausted

or not, she needed to get her own yard decorated before her neighbors gave up on her.

It had been smart to avoid dinner with Deke, and not just for his protection. She needed a hefty dose of something normal. With a smile for her decorated lamppost, she turned to face her house, thinking about what she could get done tonight. Deep down, part of her was still turning over the puzzle of who had broken into her garage and planted evidence.

The troubling thought had her whipping back around to have another look at Calder's house. The lights were up across the roofline and draped over the shrubs. While many homes on her street went with white lights, for the past three seasons Calder and Libby deferred to their young daughter and created a colorful display. The inflatable snow globe was new, as was the Santa Stop Here sign on the chimney.

Calder couldn't have done that. She'd visited with him in the hospital at lunchtime and the doctors didn't plan to release him before tomorrow. Libby was pregnant. Abby sighed. She supposed another neighbor had stepped in. Not surprising.

"You like it? I thought the stop sign was a nice touch."

Riley O'Brien had rounded the front corner of Calder's house. He gestured to the tiny white icicle lights dripping prettily from the roofline. He'd wrapped the front windows with wide ribbon as if they were packages. That trademark grin spread across his face. The sleeves of his flannel shirt were rolled up. He held a tape measure in his hands and his tool belt slung low across his lean hips. He looked exactly like the carpenter he claimed to be.

Realization dawned on her. "This is all your doing, isn't it?"

He shrugged one shoulder. "I finished work early. I was bored."

She surveyed Calder's house again. The view was safer than staring with fascinated interest at her new neighbor. "Tell me had help." After last night, she didn't like the idea of anyone working on a ladder alone. Not so close to where she lived anyway.

"Peg and Danny helped. Plus a few of the kids after the school bus dropped them off. It was a team effort."

Danny wasn't much more than a kid himself, so that made sense. "Peg?" Abby felt her jaw drop. "You're kidding." After the deep freeze she'd given Abby today, she was surprised the woman came anywhere near here. But, then, Calder was her friend, too.

"Not at all," Riley assured her. "Peg came over to take a look at the kitchen and talk flooring. She did all the gas lamps. I think she got a kick out of pitching in."

"Peg," Abby repeated dumbly. It seemed impossible that the woman had decorated anywhere near Abby's house rather than pummel it with eggs. "You're like the Pied Piper," Abby said with a shake of her head, "the way you get people to cooperate."

"The nuns said Tom Sawyer, but it's about the same, I guess." He gave another careless hitch of his shoulder.

"Nuns?" Now she was really confused.

His gaze shifted to Calder's place and back to her. "My teachers. Irish parents, remember? Catholic school's practically a requirement. Our school did a lot of community outreach like repair work and local theater. We learned early that jobs were easier when more people got involved."

"Well, it doesn't matter what they said then, I'm grateful to you now. It looks beautiful."

"I thought the street could use a mood lifter."

"You thought right."

He walked over and held up a shiny brass key. "Your

lock is repaired and the new snow shovel is right inside the door."

"Thanks," she said, pulling out her key ring. Anything to keep her from gawking at the man making such a positive impact around her town. All evidence pointed to him as an asset, one of the good guys, but she couldn't help wondering if she was being a fool to trust him so easily.

He tucked his hands into his pockets. "Any leads?"

"On which case?"

He shrugged. "Any or all of them."

"No leads on anything. At this point, I'm lucky I still have a job."

"It's not your fault Belclare is under siege."

She shook her head, tired of making zip for progress. "Under siege feels about right." Abby indulged in a heartfelt sigh. "Unfortunately."

As she'd gone through her day, his words had been in the back of her mind. Who would gain the most if she was gone or if she even backed down? There was no clear answer, but she knew he was right. The question had her considering almost everyone in town as a threat again. A position that danced on the edge of paranoia.

"How's Calder?"

She turned, feeling her lips curve in a relieved smile. "Healing quickly enough to give the nursing staff a hard time." She pulled out her phone to take a picture of his house. "He'll be thrilled when he sees this."

"Peg already did that," Riley said.

"Oh." She lowered her phone, feeling silly. "Of course she did."

"I'm sure he wouldn't mind another one. All lit up at night it's even better."

"True." She snapped the picture and sent it to Calder.

"Well, I'd better get busy with my own yard or I'll get the Grinch award."

"Seriously? They give those out?"

"Well, it's not an official thing." She raised her arms wide, indicating the whole block. "But it's real enough and I'm obviously way behind. When you live in Belclare, holiday spirit is kind of required."

"Let me help."

She waved an arm, indicating the entire block. "You've done plenty."

He looked at her house, his eyes crinkling at the corners. "You'll need a ladder."

She clenched her teeth against the memory of last night. "There are other options." She could just string lights over the bushes and around the doorway. A couple wreaths on the shutters would help. It wouldn't be an award-winning display, but it would be enough. Maybe she'd pick up an inflatable ornament this year.

"I don't think so. Whatever you have planned, you're not working out here alone. Come with me."

She automatically fell into step behind him, before she caught herself. "Wait. Who made you boss of the evening?"

When he turned, his mouth was twitching. "Which one of us is current on holiday decorating skills?"

"I have plenty of experience."

"Great. Tell me what you want done and where the decorations are stored and I'll do it for you. Even my boss says I'm the fastest guy on the team this year."

No surprise. She'd heard nothing but praise when she'd called the company and checked up on him. "Congratulations, but helping me isn't necessary."

He stopped short right in the middle of their driveways and she nearly barreled into his chest. She sort of wished she had.

"Necessary or not, that's how it's going to be, Abby."

The way he said her name made her feel like a completely different person. It made her want to step away from official roles and just be...herself. At least a slightly more relaxed version of herself. More like the person she'd been before the fallout from the drug bust.

"I wouldn't do anything differently," she said.

"Do you have a picture of how you did things before?"

"Yes, but I didn't mean the decorations," she clarified. "I was thinking about the drug bust."

He rocked back on his heels and crossed his arms. She didn't understand how he could look so comfortable in the chill of the evening in only his thermal and flannel shirts, jeans and boots. Maybe the tool belt had a heater built in. The thought that maybe *he* was the heater made her shiver.

Every time she saw him, he reinforced her growing opinion that he was a friendly, competent and kind man. The type of man a woman would be lucky to know. And that was the crux. Knowing her, being around her, could prove extremely unlucky for him. "You should just go on inside and take a break. I can handle it."

"No." He shook his head resolutely.

"Riley, please."

He leaned down into her face until they were nearly nose to nose. "You're stuck with my help. Deal with it."

She could see the flecks of gold in his brown eyes. Her gaze drifted lower, to his mouth. His lips tipped up at one corner and she forced her eyes back to his before he could tease her with that wicked grin. It didn't help. He was staring at her mouth. She licked her lips, wondering how he would kiss. Slow and easy? Quick and hard? She'd be happy with either. Both even.

She stepped back before she gave in and found out. She didn't want him to get hurt because some unidentified terrorist wanted to make her suffer. But he wasn't backing down. Did that make him foolish or her careless for appreciating it?

"Okay. Fine."

He straightened. "Glad you understand. Now, will you show me where you store the decorations?"

She tipped her head back toward the garage. "In the loft."

"All right." He walked to the bed of his truck and unlocked the storage bin on one side. "I'm grabbing a couple of work lights."

"Good idea." It would be dark as pitch in that garage loft.

She walked on back to the garage and tested out the key he'd given her for the new lock. It felt solid and worked smoothly. She expected nothing less. Everywhere he'd been in Belclare, people commented on his friendliness as well as his expertise with all kinds of odd jobs.

Inside, she flipped the switch, grateful for the light. The narrow space was big enough for her car, but she rarely parked in here, thinking it offered her neighbors a sense of security when she left the official sedan out in the driveway. After what happened to Calder, her neighbors probably felt differently now.

"Thinking about this morning?"

She wanted to kick something but checked the urge. "I don't understand why anyone would so obviously plant evidence like that."

"To get under your skin."

"Well, it's working. But I'm not letting these scumbags make me doubt what's right."

"Good." He walked past her and reached for her stepladder, carrying it over to access the loft.

The clatter of the aluminum as he opened it and the legs settling securely on the cement floor made her swear.

"You okay?"

"I'm angry." She drew in a big, deep breath. Didn't help. "Calder's an innocent bystander. Why don't they just come at me?"

"A broken lock and planted evidence sounds to me like they are," Riley said, climbing up a few rungs of the ladder until he could read the labels on the plastic boxes stored there. "Which ones do you want me to bring down?"

"The red box of wreaths and the green box of lights should do it."

"You're sure?"

"I can always add more when things settle down."

His laughter bounced around the garage. "All things considered, I wouldn't count on that happening anytime soon."

She took the red box he handed down and set it on the floor. "Meaning?"

"Don't jump all over me for stating the obvious." He propped the green box on his shoulder as he came down the ladder. "Someone wants to get even with you or at least make a point that they're above your attempts to enforce the law."

If only she could figure out who. "We've been over all the evidence in the drug bust, interviewed all the employees and anyone resembling a witness." As he replaced the ladder on the hooks, she picked up the red box and led the way out to the front yard. Riley followed with the heavier bin full of lights. "And we're no closer to unraveling who's really behind it all."

She opened the bins and pulled out the pictures she'd taken of last year's display while he plugged in the work lights.

He peered over her shoulder at the pictures, looked back at her house and then laughed.

"It looks that bad to your expert eye?" she asked, annoyed just a little.

"Not at all," he said, taking a step back. "I've just never seen anyone so—" he shrugged "—organized."

"Your dad taught you to swing a hammer—mine taught me to plan and document." His face clouded over, but before she could ask him anything, he motioned for the paper and pictures.

"You want the same setup?" He glanced from the pictures to the bins at their feet to the front of her house.

"It's simple, but pretty. No one complains." She'd thought the wreaths on the shutters had framed her Christmas tree in the front window rather nicely last year. And the lit evergreen garland around her front door tied it all together.

"All right. Give me an hour."

"I don't believe in double standards. We're doing this together." The teamwork wasn't just about safety.

"Want me to wait while you change clothes?"

"I'll just get my boots from the back door. Give me a second."

As they worked, she discovered she liked the company of the new guy in town. Give him time, she bemoaned, and he'd learn to hate her, too. Irritated with her uncharacteristic self-pity, she pulled out the garland for the door and its extension cord. She plugged it in, confirmed the lights were working and then handed the garland to him. "You should be able to reach this without the ladder."

He arched an eyebrow but followed her over and, as she'd said, centered the garland on the hook above the door frame. When it was positioned to his satisfaction, she plugged it in again and smiled. "Perfect."

"Thanks." He took a theater-worthy bow. "What's next?"

"I'll start lighting the shrubs if you hang the wreaths on the shutters."

"Deal."

Under the glare of the work lights they finished transforming her home in record time. He made a few little changes and she liked the improved overall effect. "You are good at this," she said as he packed up the work lights.

"I've had plenty of practice these past few days."

She stacked the empty bins together and returned them to the garage.

"I drove down Main Street this afternoon," she said when she found him waiting for her in the driveway. "It looks amazing, a step up from last year."

"That's what the boss asked for. I bet it's even prettier when it's lit up at night," he said. "Want to go for a drive?"

She did. Desperately. The intensity scared her. "Aren't you tired of Christmas lights and holiday displays by now?"

"Aren't you tired of police work?"

"A little," she confessed, startling a laugh out of both of them.

"Take a drive with me. I'll buy you a drink."

"Didn't you offer to fix me dinner?"

He unhooked his tool belt and stowed it in the truck. "Maybe I'll let a professional handle it tonight. I wouldn't want to overwhelm you with all my talents at once."

"You're a terrible flirt."

"So I've been told." He winked, opening the passenger door of his truck for her.

"No, I mean you're really bad at it."

"You want me to up my game?"

Yes. No. Uncertain, she pulled the door shut. When he slid into the driver's seat she said, "I don't want any games. I want you to be yourself."

"Easy enough." He stared at her for a moment that went on and on and she realized she was holding her breath. "What you see is what you get, Abby."

How did he do that? How did he make her feel so wanted

and alive with just a few words? She tried to analyze it, to view him as she might a suspect, searching for motive, but she couldn't quite pin him down. His body language screamed sincere interest, she knew that much. And yet he was utterly unflappable about the attraction sparking between them.

"I heard you had an inside tip on the shipment," he asked as they left the serenity of their street behind.

"That's the popular rumor."

"It isn't true?"

She shook her head. Telling him the truth would be stupid, but the one thing they didn't have was a fresh perspective. The man had serious people skills.

"You've met quite a few people in Belclare," she said.

"Are you saying I've met your informant?"

"I just told you there wasn't one. Why are you so curious about it?"

He outlined the steering wheel with his fingertips as they waited for a red light to change. "I'm more curious about how you operate. You're obviously dedicated to the job and that's good for the community. These threats are affecting everyone and that doesn't sit right with me. Cowards who use the innocent irritate me."

"Right there with you on that one."

"You must have some ideas on suspects."

"After what happened to Calder, I suspect the worst. Of everyone," she clarified. "It's problematic."

He turned onto Main and she seized on the distraction, admiring an elaborate new sleigh full of gifts, towed by reindeer in brilliant harnesses and flanked by decorated trees. "Wow," she whispered. "The tourists are going to eat this up."

"Wait until you see how the park turned out."

"Let's go look." She twisted around in the seat, hoping to catch a glimpse as they passed the intersection.

"Right after we eat. The decorations will be there all month."

RILEY WAS A little surprised Abby didn't argue more as he found an open parking space in the lot behind the pub he'd checked out a couple of nights ago. He shut off the truck's engine and pulled the key from the ignition. Before he could reach for his door, she stopped him, her hand light on his arm. He frowned. "What's wrong?"

"Just think it through," she answered. "You've said you want to stay in Belclare."

He nodded. "Right. I showed you the signed lease."

"That's my point, Riley. Having dinner with me could create long-term problems for you."

His thoughts turned dark at the implication. A woman with her stellar record and dedication shouldn't have to put up with this kind of crap. Not from the community and not from the lowlifes who wanted to exploit her concern for that community. "Are you hungry?"

"Yes," she said, her mouth curving into a soft smile. "But I have plenty of food at home."

He wondered what she'd do if he just kissed her the way he wanted to. His feelings were unexpected and unprofessional, but that didn't lessen the desire. Thinking about the way she'd looked at him earlier, he considered capitalizing on a relationship to stay close to her, but if she ever discovered his real identity and purpose it would hurt her. He didn't know her well, but he could tell she put stock in honesty and even his secrets were lies.

Tell her the truth, a voice echoed in the back of his mind. He wished it were that simple.

She didn't deserve the shock and pain of discovering

what he was. Or rather, what he wasn't. He didn't want to give her any more reasons to second-guess her instincts. He didn't want to be one more source of anxiety and disappointment.

"Well, too bad," he said resolutely. "We're here now. It's not my business what other people think any more than it's theirs what I think or do."

"It's not just what they think—"

"It's what the people behind the threats will do. I get it."

"And you don't care?"

"Oh, I care." It surprised him how much he cared. About his job, her, even Belclare as a whole. "I've been in stressful situations before."

"Care to elaborate?"

"Not out here." He shot her another grin, the one he'd learned distracted her. It worked again, as her eyes landed like a caress on his lips. "I'll be fine, Abby, no matter the fallout."

She was right. Heads turned as they entered the pub and found a small table near the scarred oak bar. "That thing could use some attention," he said.

"I think they call it character."

"Yeah, well, sometimes people forget the 'care' part of character."

A smile bloomed on her face. "Are you set on remodeling the whole town?" she asked after the waitress took their drink order.

"Of course not. Fixing things is just in my blood."

She seemed to mull over that statement for a moment before firing the next question. "Will your parents visit? I'm sure they'd be thrilled with what you've done."

He was granted a short reprieve as their drinks and a basket of the pub's hand-cut potato chips arrived. Lying was critical to his success here. It was absolutely essential to keeping her safe and finding the culprits behind the threats. So why was he fighting it so hard?

He steered the conversation to simpler topics while he stewed over his predictable nature. This need for attachment and approval had been a problem for as long as he could remember.

He understood it was a product of being an orphan with no clear understanding of his real past. Making up his history had been amusing and no one knew enough to correct his theories. Some days he'd been the son of humble farmers, other days he had superhero blood in his veins.

In no small measure, he'd found a working solution as one of Director Casey's Specialists. He'd become part of a professional family where the past didn't matter. Together, learning from the best operatives and support techs, they'd been able to accomplish tasks other law enforcement teams couldn't.

Now he was out here on his own. An island once more. Casey had asked him to think this through. Riley wondered if his mentor had anticipated this sort of emotional blowback.

"What's bothering you?"

He looked up from his plate into Abby's concerned face. "Just thinking about my parents," he said. It was true enough. Being an adult didn't change his curiosity about where he'd come from. "You're right. They would be proud of the work I've done here."

She smiled. "Will you invite them?"

"You just want more tourist traffic," he teased. "I've sent pictures. They don't travel much this time of year." Riley didn't want to think about the kind of failure that would bring his professional parent, Thomas Casey, to Belclare.

"You'll have to let me know what they think."

"Sure."

From her purse, he heard her phone chime. "Do you have them send those 24/7?"

"Right now I do. Just a traffic dispatch." She leaned forward, lowering her voice. "I'm worried about this weekend. We received threats against specific targets today."

"They damn well better not mess with our display in the park. I worked hard on that."

Her smile didn't quite reach her eyes. "The park. The police station. The docks. Homeland Security called me again, but I don't have anything new to tell them."

"If they're so worried, they should send you some manpower."

Her eyes went wide and her head bobbed up and down. "That's what I said. Belclare citizens check out. I know it has to be someone close, but I've turned over every stone and double-checked every rumor. We aren't getting closer."

"You will."

"After what happened to Calder...well, I can't help but think of worst-case scenarios."

"That's natural."

"I know. Deke's publicity efforts likely saved opening weekend, but I don't want some sick group turning the happy crowds into victims and ruining everything."

He reached over and caught her hand. "People are resilient. Even if the worst happens, the town will rally behind you."

"More likely they'll rally with cheers and confetti at my going-away party."

"I don't believe that. Everyone I talk to likes you."

She narrowed her gaze, assessed him. "You're lying."

He cleared his throat. "I didn't say they liked your victory speech."

"Nice," she said, pulling her hand away as if she just realized they were touching. *In public.*

"I don't know much about your line of work, but if you ever need someone to bounce theories off, I can listen."

"Thanks."

He heard the sincerity in that single word and wished he could offer her more assurances. His own searches into the backgrounds of those who were most outspoken hadn't turned up any clear connection to known terrorists.

Everyone at the top said this was a sleeper cell. If it was true, whoever they'd planted here in Belclare had been provided with a rock-solid cover. He didn't care for the grim parallel that made to his situation. The food arrived and he decided to forget work long enough for them to actually enjoy what they'd come here for—dinner.

"Great." She stared at her phone, looking like someone had sucker punched her.

"More trouble?" His senses went on alert.

"You could say that. They found a match for the DNA on my snow shovel."

"Can you talk about it?"

"I probably shouldn't." She swiped at her phone, then raised her blue eyes to meet his. "It appears to have been used against a guy with a long and impressive rap sheet."

"Someone in Belclare has an impressive rap sheet?"

"No." She scowled at her phone another minute or two while he wolfed down more of his burger. "This guy's current address is a morgue in Baltimore. Preliminary cause of death is head trauma."

Alarms went off in Riley's mind. The implications of that were pretty dangerous for her.

"I should get to the office." She looked longingly at her plate, clearly irritated by the idea of leaving her dinner unfinished. "I love these burgers, but my appetite is gone." She grimaced and tossed her phone back into her purse.

"It won't wait until morning?"

She shook her head. "I need to head this off with the Baltimore P.D."

He agreed 100 percent. Someone was trying to set her up for murder. The why was an easy guess. If she was in legal trouble it would get her out of the way. But who needed her out of the way and what did they have planned when they succeeded? Planting evidence of a crime was a potential goal of its own. Make the chief look guilty and muddy her reputation, lessen the *good* and the impact of her big takedown.

That effort would prove impotent. Abby was one of the most recognized and respected people in town. Unless time of death was the middle of the night, it was likely someone in Belclare could offer her an alibi. As her neighbor, he could easily vouch for the times that her car came and went from the driveway between their houses.

"Are you worried?"

Her blue eyes narrowed at him. "Are you asking if I did it?"

He snorted. "I know you didn't do it."

She leaned back and crossed her arms over her chest. "Care to explain how it is you're so certain? I haven't even given you any details."

"I don't need them. You live next door and I'm a light sleeper." He leaned closer. "I'm using the bedroom on that side of the house. Your car didn't go anywhere last night."

"You didn't happen to hear anyone busting open my garage and stealing my shovel, did you?"

"No," he confessed with a shake of his head. "They managed that sometime after I left for work."

"You think they wanted me to find it."

He shrugged. "Sure. It was a hassle for you, this morning, right?"

"It was a violation," she said, her voice hard. "Something like this could cost me my job, whether or not I'm innocent."

"Just proves my point. Whoever did it got to you, threw a wrench in your schedule, and now that you have a body to go along with the bloody shovel you have a serious, ongoing distraction from your responsibilities in Belclare."

"For a guy who's just passing through you seem to have your finger on the pulse around here."

He grinned at her. "I keep telling you I like your town. When will you believe me?"

She winced. "It may not be my town much longer."

"That's doubtful. You don't strike me as the type to go down without a fight." He winked at her. "I've seen the video that proves it."

Those bright blue eyes rolled up to the ceiling. "If I could go back in time and tell myself to shut up, I would."

He laughed. "And miss all this fun?"

A fire truck went roaring past the pub and her phone rang again.

She pulled it out of her bag, but when she read the message, all the blood drained from her face. "The police station's on fire."

He caught the waitress's attention and signaled for the check. "Let's get you over there."

"I can walk."

"Absolutely not." It might be the opening her enemies were looking for. Tossing cash onto the table, he escorted her through the pub with a hand at the small of her back.

Her poise and self-control impressed him. She carried her head high, her stride easy, but he felt the tension in her rigid posture and the tight muscles under his fingertips. Any more stressful surprises would break another person, but he didn't think Abby would snap. Not now, not ever. While he admired her fortitude, he worried that her unyielding nature would only push the culprits behind this threat to up the ante. His concerns were justified as they reached the police station and found the end of the building closest to the employee parking area engulfed in flames.

"Some days I long for a world without YouTube," she said as he parked across the street, well away from the responding firefighters.

"If the problem is a terrorist cell within Belclare, YouTube is irrelevant," he pointed out. He turned, feeling her intense gaze on him. "What?"

"Again, not sounding like a typical construction worker."

He shrugged that off. "I can read and I listen to the news. Besides, between the sign, the internet and your mention of Homeland Security, I'd have to be an ostrich not to come to that conclusion."

"Of course."

He'd made her wary again. Damn it. She was a smart woman and she must be picking up on more than his ability to connect a few dots between the details she had started to confide. "If you have questions for me I'll answer them." With the cover story, of course. This entire operation was about keeping her safe. To do that, he had to gain her trust.

She tore her gaze from the fire to study him. "I believe you would." She opened the door. "But those questions will have to wait."

He tagged along as she marched toward the fire chief supervising the process of dousing the flames. The fire chief kept her at a safe distance and, after a brief exchange, urged her toward the other cops who'd been unwillingly evicted from the police station. But she didn't move, remaining apart and scowling at the blaze lapping along the roof.

"Did he tell you anything?"

"Only that they'll have it contained shortly."

"Good to know."

Her fury was obvious. What she intended to do about it, not so much. She didn't need speculation or suggestions from the new guy in town. He couldn't decide what to do, other than his job. "I'll take you home when you're ready."

"I'm not going anywhere until the building is secure."

"I figured as much."

She finally pulled her gaze away from the fire. "You don't have to wait. One of the officers can take me home."

"Waiting isn't a problem."

After another minute or two, she stalked over to the officers who'd been ousted from their building. Riley stayed put, having a pretty good idea of how that conversation would go. Instead of following her, which felt a little clingy and intrusive, he scanned the bystanders, looking for anything remotely suspicious. Spotting Mr. Filmore standing on the other side of the fire trucks, he headed that way.

"Hello, Mr. Filmore," he said, hand extended.

The man squinted at him from behind his glasses. "Who—? Oh. You're that decorator fellow."

"That's me." Riley pushed his hands into his pockets, not surprised that Mr. Filmore refused to shake hands. People didn't come wound any tighter than the man who obsessed about the historic accuracy of every snowflake in Belclare.

"Why are you here?"

Riley wanted to ask him the same question. "I was grabbing dinner at the pub and heard the commotion." No sense giving him any ammunition to use against Abby later.

"Were you in the building?"

"Yes, of course," Filmore said, wringing his hands. "I had another issue to discuss with Chief Jensen."

"Is everything settled with the welcome sign?" It had been on the project board for this afternoon, but Riley had been with a different team at the park.

"As much as can be expected," Filmore groused. "She

has to *do* something!" He turned abruptly, the fire and emergency lights casting grim shadows across his pinched features. "This eyesore is intolerable."

Exactly what did the man think Abby should do? Apologize to the criminals and terrorists? Grab a fire hose? "You'll be surprised how fast we can clean things up. I'll pitch in. Will you?"

Filmore ignored him. "This season is doomed to fail. Belclare may never recover."

"The rest of the town looks fantastic," Riley said. "I bet Chief Jensen is already planning how to keep everyone safe for Saturday's opening."

"I know your type," Filmore said, shifting to put himself toe-to-toe with Riley. "Every year it takes more of you than last year. You say the right things, but you don't care."

Riley opened his mouth, but Filmore was on a roll.

"That building is eighty years old. I've personally overseen every so-called improvement of the past twenty-some years." The garish lights emphasized Filmore's wild eyes. "This is an unmitigated disaster all because of her!" He flung his arm in Abby's direction. "She talks safety but she's a hypocrite. That building does not deserve to suffer."

The man was starting to sound a little warped to Riley. "Take it easy, Mr. Filmore."

"Take it easy? She is single-handedly destroying this town."

Riley fought the urge to put the man out of everyone's misery. Two quiet punches and Mr. Filmore could rethink his priorities while his body learned how to function again.

Moving Filmore up on his list of potential suspects, Riley muttered some soothing nonsense in an attempt to calm the man down. Just when he thought he was making progress, Filmore launched into another tirade.

Before Riley could steer her away, Abby walked right

into Filmore's outburst. He pushed Riley aside and starting shouting at her.

"This is *your* fault!"

"Mr. Filmore—" she put a hand on his shoulder "—are you okay?"

He shrugged her off. "Absolutely not!"

"Would you like me to call over a paramedic?" She gave Riley a look to do it anyway.

Incensed, Mr. Filmore put himself right in her face and it took all of Riley's self-control to abide by Abby's signal to step back and let the man blow. He didn't know how Abby put up with Filmore's increasingly outrageous accusations.

"Mr. Filmore," she said when he paused for air. "I am sorry for your distress. I know how much Belclare means to you."

"You are a failure! This city has never been more unsafe. Opening weekend is ruined! The people of this town deserve better than you."

Riley moved to intervene, ready to protect either Filmore or Abby. He wasn't sure which one would need him more. The last thing he expected was for Abby to slip her arm through Mr. Filmore's as if they were the best of friends. "I understand your concern. Have you seen the park yet?"

"Of course."

"I think the decorating crew outdid themselves. Were you pleased?"

"Yes. But at this rate it will all go up in smoke tomorrow."

Riley trailed after them, unwilling to leave her alone with a nut like Filmore. Riley might suggest she keep a few of the guys he'd been working with in town as extra security. He couldn't be sure she'd accept the idea, but it could resolve part of her manpower issue. For two blocks, he considered ideas and solutions and what he had to share in his next report for Director Casey, and then they rounded the corner and all three of them stopped.

Memorial Park sat like a jewel in the heart of Belclare. The scent of fresh greenery laced the cold air and out here, the burning police station might as well be on a different planet. Logically, he knew it was the breeze from the water blowing the acrid smoke in the opposite direction, but the effect was stunning.

"Isn't this lovely, Mr. Filmore? It looks just like those pictures from the 1940s."

"It does," he allowed, his voice tight. "The decorators did well here."

Riley kept his mouth shut so he wouldn't blow the progress Abby was making.

"I agree." Abby's voice was steady and calm in the brittle air. "Tourists will love this, they'll flock here, taking pictures and making memories. Belclare will be fine."

"But the burned-out station is an eyesore," he moaned.

"You know what I didn't see at the station?"

"What?"

"I didn't see any flames on the front of the building."

Riley realized she was right. The roof had been burning as well as the back, but the facade hadn't been on fire. In fact the displays in front of the building were mostly intact.

"The police department may have to take up temporary residence at Sadie's for a few days," Abby offered, "but at first glance the tourists won't know the difference."

"You sound so sure," Filmore mumbled.

"I am. The buildings you protect so well, the structures you speak for, were here long before either of us. Thanks to your dedication, they will be here long after we're gone. Tonight's setback notwithstanding."

"You're right. I'm sorry I lost my temper."

Riley was sure he heard tears in Filmore's voice.

"These have been trying times," she added graciously, "but we'll get through it. Together."

Filmore stopped short in the middle of the sidewalk and Riley braced for trouble.

"Yes, it will take both of us to get this done," Filmore agreed. He reached over and covered her gloved hand with his. "Belclare means so much to me, Chief Jensen. My apologies."

Riley didn't like the tone and his mind ran off in conspiratorial directions over Filmore's phrasing.

But Abby just smiled at the older man. "Sometimes those things that mean the most drive us to do things we never dreamed ourselves capable of doing," she said.

"There are times for extreme measures."

"Yes." She turned them back toward Main Street, back toward the mess and destruction of the fire.

Riley noticed how the Belclare police officers had managed to spread out at even intervals, on both sides of the street.

"Sometimes when we care so much about a cause, we're willing to hurt the people and places we love," she continued.

Filmore flinched and tried to pull free of Abby's grip, but she held firm. "I don't know what you mean," he protested. "Release me."

"Mr. Filmore, I can't do that." With her free hand, she motioned to one of the men across the street. "Martin Filmore, you are under arrest for arson."

She started to read him his rights, but he interrupted. "Stop this at once. This is absurd." He rubbed his gloved hands together. "I—I was in the police station when the fire started."

"So I've been told," she said, and then continued reading his rights.

"Chief Jensen, I love that old building. You know I could never do such a heinous thing."

Riley noticed tears rolling down the older man's cheeks as he was crying in earnest now. The denials were tumbling free. If Filmore was guilty, he did a fine job portraying an emotionally distraught innocent bystander. He would have to send this up the line to Director Casey immediately.

"I know you'd never want to." Abby let him ramble as another officer stepped up to cuff him and help him gently into the back of a cruiser. With the police station on fire, where they would question him was anyone's guess.

When Filmore was gone and the firefighters finished a final walk-through, Abby returned to the truck. "You stayed."

He opened the passenger door for her. "Said I would."

"I appreciate it."

"No problem." He closed her door and walked around the hood, slid in behind the steering wheel. Throughout the ordeal, she hadn't shown any of the weariness she clearly felt now. "Why did you arrest him?"

"The officers on duty said he was squirrely and he kept eyeing my office where they believe the fire started."

Riley's jaw clenched. Everyone in town knew she frequently worked late. Did she realize Filmore might've killed her? And if she hadn't been in the office, starting the fire there would reflect badly on her, further damaging her reputation.

"On top of those circumstantial points," she continued, "he'd been at the station this morning for a meeting about the graffiti. He had access to the office and he doesn't usually bother me twice in one week, much less in a day."

Riley thought about the detonators. "Did you see him plant anything in your office?"

"No, but I was effectively distracted by a few other issues."

"Filmore strikes me as a high-maintenance kind of guy."

"If he did set the fire, and that seems likely, that makes him the kind of guy who's managed to deceive me for years." He heard the sorrow in her voice, knew she was wondering who else was fooling her. "While I'm happy to remove a problem, it's hard to wrap my head around the idea that Filmore was arranging drug deals and hurling those other threats at me."

"I can't see him toppling Calder's ladder," Riley said.

"Agreed."

"What's next?" She looked so tired he wished he could take her home.

"First a warrant for Filmore's house," she explained, her voice weary. "Then, as soon as we have any real evidence, I'll have to write up something for the feds."

"Do you want me to take you to Filmore's?"

"No. They don't need me hovering. My officers are good at what they do." She sighed and leaned her head back against the seat. "Right now I just want to get home and sink into a tub full of bubbles."

Well, there was an image that would be haunting him all night. Developments and reports could only offer so much distraction from the thought of Abby's naked body covered only by fragile bubbles. Right next door. At least, she was calling it a night. A good night's sleep would go a long way. Not that he'd be getting any shut-eye.

There were other questions he could ask, but he kept them to himself. He didn't want to pile on any more than he already had, even in the role of curious neighbor. He would leave the nosing around to Mrs. Wilks. For tonight anyway.

Arresting Filmore, admitting Homeland Security might be right about a homegrown terrorist cell operating in Belclare wouldn't be easy developments for Abby to accept. This was her town, after all. No one wanted to believe they didn't recognize evil when they saw it.

But Riley knew for certain that evil was sometimes the last suspect on the list.

Chapter Nine

The comfortable silence on the drive home soothed Abby, offering a blissful relief after the noise of the firefighters, the concerns of her officers and the erratic ramblings of Filmore. She hoped the search warrant turned up something conclusive and useful. As much as she hated the idea that Martin Filmore had fooled her all these years, it would be news to celebrate and reassure her town, as well as the tourists they hoped would come out for the weekend.

As a police officer, and now as a chief, nothing felt worse than knowing the community questioned their general safety. Sure, life involved some measure of risk, but when people doubted the ability of their law enforcement, things had a tendency to spiral out of control.

"Want to talk about it?"

She looked across the seat to her new neighbor who'd made himself her chauffeur for the evening. "I'd rather not."

"If that changes, you know where to find me."

Did she ever. Last night had been bad enough with images of him following her into sleep and all through her dreams. Had she ever been so infatuated? Not as an adult.

Waking with Riley O'Brien on her mind had been a delicious start to the day. She could tell from the way her pulse skipped and danced when she saw him that the situation wasn't likely to resolve anytime soon. Not without some sort of acknowledgment or action. But this was the worst time to entertain the idea of a new relationship or even friends with benefits.

When he pulled into the driveway, Abby tried to summon the strength to get out of the car. She wanted a shower first to get the smoke out of her hair, then a long soak in a bubble bath. She might leave her coat on the rail outside the kitchen door so it could air out. Mr. Filmore had attacked her police station. Specifically her office. She didn't need spray paint and graffiti to understand the significance and potential deadly consequences.

At least he'd failed on that count, she thought as another wave of relief washed over her. No one had been injured. That was one positive point in this mess.

But something had pushed Filmore to act against what he held most dear and set fire to a piece of history. Hopefully, the interrogation and search would provide a solid direction. Her gut said Filmore was simply a cog in a wheel, but if that was true, who was calling the shots? Who had the leverage to push Filmore over the edge?

It seemed impossible that she was considering people she had known for years.

What she needed was a better lead, but neither the evidence nor her instincts were cooperating at the moment.

"Hey." Riley snagged her attention with a soft tap on her shoulder. "Are you the fake or real type?"

With all that had happened, somehow the question grated on her last nerve. She glared at him. "What kind of question is that?"

He leaned back, lifting his hand from her shoulder. "Ease up, Abby. I was referring to Christmas trees."

"Oh!" She wanted to laugh and shake free of the constant edginess plaguing her, but she couldn't quite pull it off. "I have a fake one in the attic that I'll pull down when

I get a chance. The idea of wandering through a Christmas tree lot…" Her voice trailed off.

"You've received threats about shopping for Christmas trees?"

She reached for the door handle, immediately regretting the careless words. Overtired, she wouldn't be any good to anyone. Based on the muttering, Riley was offended by the idea of that kind of threat. "Not exactly." She shouldn't tell him anything and yet she suddenly wanted to talk about all of it. She wanted to unburden herself, even if he was basically a stranger.

Maybe *because* he was a stranger. He wouldn't have any preconceived notions about what should and shouldn't bother her.

There had been ridiculous, silly threats that were obviously from lunatics piling on to her sudden notoriety. And there had been the more direct threats from people who either knew firsthand or had researched Belclare's annual traditions. "It's not a big deal."

"No? I think I'd disagree if you told me the truth."

She forced her lips into a reassuring smile. "It was a silly one," she managed. Why could she be so strong for the people in her department and hold her ground with the likes of Mayor Scott and Mr. Filmore but not with Riley?

With Riley she was too ready to confess her weaknesses and worries. Though she wouldn't change a thing about her decisions, she had the irrational urge to discuss those decisions with him. He triggered some tiny, long-forgotten part of her that trusted people. The part of her she'd shut down in favor of navigating the boys' club that was law enforcement. Taking over as chief in Belclare had been a step up the career ladder, but the welcoming people here had given her a significant measure of relief, as well. Her officers and support staff served Belclare with pride, accepting her easily enough. That didn't mean she burdened them with the thoughts or concerns that fell on her shoulders.

Until the drug bust, she hadn't needed to. Her role as police chief came with a burden of responsibility that she carried willingly and easily. Previously, the most serious crime in Belclare had been the occasional petty theft or bar fight. She wouldn't allow that reputation for safety to change. Not on her watch and especially not during the tourist season that buoyed the town from year to year.

Riley had been kind and supportive, but she would do well to remember she didn't really know him.

"You're thinking too deeply again."

She blinked. He was in front of her—he had, in fact, left the driver's seat and come around to open her door while her mind had been skipping around. She glanced at the empty driver's seat and back to where he stood now.

"Come on." He held out a hand to help her. "I'll walk you in."

Did he think she'd get lost between the drive and the door? Was he worried she'd turn into his kitchen rather than her own? Now, that was a tempting thought. She put her hand in his, knowing before they touched that his skin would be warm, his palm rough from work. "I was going to tell you." She just hadn't decided if she'd tell him her professional troubles or her intimate, personal desires.

"So tell me." He gave her fingers a gentle squeeze, encouraging her to move, but she stayed in the seat.

The view was striking, the moment weighted with significance as her heart pounded in her chest. Surely he could hear it, too. She reached out, wiping away the smudge of soot near his hairline. Filled with need and raw awareness, she wanted to simultaneously rush forward and stop time as she leaned close and pressed her lips to his.

He didn't respond. His hand, fingers warm around hers, didn't even twitch.

Stupid. Idiot. The internal reprimand continued as she pulled back, searching for the right words. There had to be some lighthearted phrase that could explain away her unwelcome blunder into his personal space. She might have to move. Out of the neighborhood. She'd go find a hotel if he'd just let her go.

Hysterical laughter bubbled in her chest, but she smothered it. This kiss might just succeed where all of the criminal threats and fallout from the drug bust had failed. The impetuous kiss might drive her right out of Belclare. "Excuse me." She didn't know where to go. He remained rooted in place, blocking the logical way out of the truck.

She tried to decide if she could slide across the bench seat and out the driver's door and still maintain her dignity. Of course her dignity had taken flight during that brief one-sided kiss. She'd misinterpreted his kindness as a reflection of her attraction. How…totally stupid. She was too weary to come up with a better word. Good grief, she was a fool. How had her intuition failed her so badly?

Why didn't he say anything? She frowned at their joined hands. Why wouldn't he let go of her?

"Excuse me," she repeated, shocked that it was even possible for her to feel increasingly humiliated with every passing second. She shifted, trying to scoot away from that strange, bewildered expression on his face. Trying to escape the mortifying moment.

"Wait." The single word he uttered sounded strained.

She froze, too embarrassed to look at him.

"Abby."

"Mmm-hmm?"

"You surprised me."

"Okay. Sorry." She winced as the apology tumbled from

her lips. This wasn't like her. None of this was like her. "Thanks for your help. Have a nice—"

She gasped as he tugged her back to the edge of the seat. He pulled her knees to either side of his trim hips and linked his hands at the small of her back. His breath fanned softly against her skin, mingling with her own as he leaned close enough that his lips were on hers. Light at first, then a claiming that sent her pulse into overdrive.

Her hands fisted in the front of his vest and she hung on for dear life. The kiss spun out, sweeping her away as his tongue stroked into her mouth. She tasted the smoky air, the lingering pepper of the fries and the unique flavor of him. She wrapped her legs around him, her heart racing. Relief and desire were a heady mix as the embarrassment of moments ago was blasted away by this passionate flare.

"You surprised me," he repeated, this time against her cheek.

"Remind me to do it more often," she said, nipping gently at his jaw. "You have an interesting response."

He chuckled, pulling her close enough to feel his arousal. His brown eyes glinted in the weak light cast by the lamp in the cab.

"Oh." She dropped her head to his shoulder. "Anyone might see us out here." Obviously she'd lost all of her powers of common sense when it came to Riley O'Brien.

"So come inside with me." His wide palms cruised up and down her back, his fingers sliding under the clasp of her bra. "I have cookies."

"I can't do that," she replied, though she'd be hard-pressed to come up with a logical excuse right this second.

"Then your place. We'll skip the cookies."

She laughed. "No. Not there, either."

He kissed her again and she nearly relented. "All right."

He reached up and flicked the switch, plunging the truck into darkness. "It's a challenge, but I can make it work here."

She should've found that offensive, but all she could do was laugh. She couldn't remember anyone in her past who made her laugh, who made her feel as lighthearted as Riley did. "You really don't waste time."

His mouth was warm and tender as he trailed kisses across her cheek to her ear. "You knew that," he murmured.

She let the words shiver through her, let her head fall back, granting him full access to her throat. A warm feeling bloomed in her chest, something more than the passion he stoked with his sensual touches. Yes, she did know that about him. At the moment, she appreciated it.

Not enough people were willing to be so honest about what they wanted. He wanted her—the physical evidence was clear on that. She wanted him, too, but she couldn't bring herself to satisfy this rush of lust in his truck in full view of her neighbors or the patrol car assigned to the neighborhood. Mayor Scott would have a field day using a public indecency ticket against her in the next town council meeting.

She pushed at his shoulders. "Hey, are you trying to kill my career?"

"What?"

"There's a morality clause in my contract." He fluttered kisses along the sensitive skin of her neck and she giggled. "Stop." She pushed at him again, taking every millimeter of space he reluctantly gave her to gather herself. "Seriously. Stop."

"I have to?"

"Yes. For the moment."

He grumbled but eased back. The cold air was bracing, but it wouldn't cool down the all-consuming heat she felt deep inside. That unquenchable fire could only be satisfied by the man in front of her.

"I'm not teasing you," she said, wanting to be as direct and clear as he'd been with her.

His brow furrowed. "I didn't say you were."

"Good. I just, um, wanted to get that out in the open. I, *ah*—" she pushed at her hair "—want this to happen. Just not tonight. Not out here."

"I'm all for a warmer venue." He put his hands to her waist and boosted her out of the truck, letting her body slide down his in a slow, delicious caress. "I'll walk you to the door."

He nearly destroyed her resolve with that smoldering gaze and hot, strong body so ready for her. "You're a walking temptation," she accused.

"Same goes." He paused, one boot on the bottom step, his hand catching her coat sleeve. "I'm right next door."

She felt her lips curve. "Trust me, I'm aware."

"I don't like the idea of you being alone tonight."

"There are certain disadvantages," she said, dragging a fingertip along the rough stubble of his jaw. "But I'll manage."

He cupped her palm to his lips. "Lock your doors."

She almost gave in. "You, too." But he didn't let her go at that.

RILEY STARED INTO those wide blue eyes, his blood running hot, but it wasn't all about those kisses. He was furious about the fire and more than a little concerned about the evidence on the shovel. The more he thought about it, the more likely he decided it had been an attempt on her life—at the very least on her freedom.

It was hard to believe Filmore had taken that leap on his own. Was one person planning all of these stunts? Or were they up against more than one threat? And how long before this nebulous enemy tried again?

The smart thing was to take a step back and be clear about the situation, despite what his body wanted. This was a razor's edge he was dancing on and he didn't want to ever give her cause to doubt him or his motives toward her.

He didn't expect to be drawn so strongly to Abby on a personal level, but she captivated him. From her consistent strength and determination through the adversity to her passionate kisses.

"How will emergencies get handled tonight?" With the police station closed, it was the perfect opportunity for someone to strike. His gaze roamed the shadows, searching for threats.

"Everything's handled, Riley. I'll be fine."

He wanted to believe her. "Let me sleep on your couch."

"No. The couch isn't big enough for both of us." Her smile was as loaded as her words. "I need quiet more than…"

He stepped back. It was easy enough to fill in the blanks. Tonight had left him with plenty of business to take care of before morning. "Give me your phone."

That sultry smile still teasing her lips, she pulled it out of her pocket and placed it in his palm. He added his name and number to her contacts and returned it.

"Keep your phone close."

She nodded her agreement before pulling away from his touch. He waited while she went inside. Walking backward, watching her at the window, he crossed over to his back door. Every gut instinct he had said leaving her alone was the wrong thing to do.

Whatever was happening, whoever was behind all this, it felt as if they were getting closer to the goal of destroying her with every passing hour.

She gave a little wave as she locked her back door. He returned it just before she dropped the curtain back in place. He noticed she'd left her coat on the back step to air out. Following her example, he removed his vest and slung it over the handrail.

But when he went to pull his screen door shut, it wouldn't latch. Something was caught under the door near the hinges.

Squeezing through the narrowed opening, he used his phone as a flashlight and saw the problem: a wool scarf.

It looked familiar, but it didn't smell like Abby's bright citrus fragrance and he'd never seen her wear anything in the soft pastel colors. Mrs. Wilks would know who it belonged to, she had the pulse of the whole neighborhood, but Riley didn't want to disturb her at this hour. He had more pressing matters to deal with.

He grabbed a beer, sipping at it slowly while he waited for his laptop to warm up. As much as he wanted to stare out of the side windows toward Abby's house, he resisted. Director Casey had tasked him with protecting her and Riley wasn't convinced Filmore was the end of the threat. The violent messages on the sign had promised a more expansive fallout for Abby as well as the citizens of Belclare. A few acts of vandalism, he suspected, were only the beginning.

While they would certainly be affected if their police chief was injured, killed or simply removed, most people of Belclare wouldn't suffer specifically. What in the hell was the ultimate plan and who was so damned determined to make Abby pay?

AT ELEVEN HE WENT OUT and turned off the Christmas lights. The patrol car drove by on the cross street as he lingered at the front door, watching as the displays winked into darkness up and down the street.

Only Abby's lights stayed on. He thought of her upstairs in her bathtub, her skin warm and rosy under the layer of bubbles. A quick rush of troubling what-if scenarios flashed through his mind and just when he'd decided to grab his pistol from the kitchen, her door opened and she stepped out into the cold night air to turn off her lights.

She was cute as all get out in a thick robe, her hair piled high on her head. It was too easy to imagine how she'd emerged from the tub, dried off that amazing body and tucked herself into that warm robe. Only his training kept him in place when every fiber of his being longed to race across the short distance, scoop her into his arms and carry her up to bed—hers or his, didn't matter.

That would be one way to be sure no one hurt her tonight. He needed to protect her. Protect the city. Better not to blow the long game with a shortsighted leap that could backfire and hurt them both. Between her trust issues and his lies, the odds were stacked against them, even without the people trying to oust her or murder her.

After she'd gone back in, Riley did the same and finished his report, bringing Director Casey up to speed. Feeling like a slacker for not making more progress identifying targets, he ended the email with a recommendation to take a closer look into Filmore's past. His sources in Belclare hadn't given him much to go on, though that might change as news spread of the man's arrest.

On the den floor, Riley laid out maps of the city given to him by the decorating company. What value did Belclare offer terrorists? It was a friendly community. Small and close-knit. Putting a sleeper cell here didn't make sense.

There was the proximity to Baltimore and even Washington, D.C. The docks on the Chesapeake Bay offered easy access up and down the Eastern Seaboard, but that only explained the drug traffic.

"Why plant terrorists here?" Riley laced his fingers behind his head. "What's the attraction?"

The docks? The Christmas Village? Other than those two things, the only claim to fame was the recluse artist who'd been devoted enough to Belclare to speak out on the morning shows urging people to visit the Christmas Village.

Riley let out a frustrated groan. He was going in circles. His best guesses were getting him nowhere. He considered Filmore nothing more than a whiny snob, but the man had set fire to an historical landmark.

"What am I missing?" He mulled over the question as he put away the maps and tossed the beer bottle into the recycling bin. His best hope at this hour was a revelation in his sleep. The boss wanted him down at the warehouse early tomorrow and showing up sluggish would do more harm than good. For both of his jobs.

He might not have identified the threat, but he could feel it, just out of sight, waiting to strike.

Chapter Ten

Friday, December 2, 8:45 a.m.

Abby's gaze drifted from the laptop to her cell phone. She'd called in at six to check on things and decided both she and her officers would be more effective if she worked from home today. With the reporters dogging her every step, it was best if she stayed out of the way.

Besides, she didn't want any witnesses to her persistent daydreams. Even with an in-box full of more dire and personal threats, she couldn't get her mind off Riley's kisses.

The man had skills that went far beyond hanging garland and looking hot in a tool belt. The first thing she'd done this morning was check the driveway, hoping for a glimpse of him, but his truck was gone.

So she'd called in and tried to focus on being chief of police—a job which, according to today's overwhelmed in-box, she was failing miserably. In the meetings following the drug bust, both FBI and Homeland Security agents had told her to hand the bulk of this off to someone in her department. They'd had good reasons and she didn't doubt their experience. But she'd taken a look at her small department and just couldn't saddle any of her officers with this kind of mess.

She'd been at it long enough now that she recognized

the spam and lunatics, easily weeding them out before she forwarded messages she thought were valid on up to the federal analysts. Belclare didn't have the cyber forensic experts to follow the bread crumbs to something helpful.

She was making her second pot of coffee when her doorbell rang. Hoping it might be Mrs. Wilks with cookies, she hurried to the door. Flowers filled her peephole, an arrangement large enough that it hid the face of the deliveryman.

Mrs. Wilks would've come to the back. Cautious now, she opened the door. "Yes?"

"Delivery for Chief Jensen."

She smiled, recognizing Deke's cultured voice behind the green floral tissue paper. "What are you doing?" She opened the door wider and invited him in.

"I thought you deserved something beautiful after the recent trouble," he said, handing her the vase.

The scent of lilies and roses filled her front room as she set the arrangement on her coffee table. She unwrapped the protective tissue and marveled at the flowers and the crystal vase.

"For a shy, artistic celebrity, you're spending a great deal of time out and about," she said.

"For a police chief you seem to be spending a great deal of time in the field," he countered.

Fair point. "Would you like coffee?"

"No, thank you. I can't stay long." He removed his cap and gloves and settled into the wing chair facing her. "How bad is the station?"

"It's not destroyed, which is a plus. And they tell me it's possible that no one will know the difference from the front."

"Clever arsonist. Are you sure you have the right man?"

She nodded sadly. "I've seen the video. Filmore cried throughout his confession."

"He does love all of this old architecture."

"He does," she agreed. "We're still trying to sort out what drove him over the edge."

"How fortunate you were nearby to get him off the streets."

She rubbed her palms together as she gathered her thoughts. Guilt nipped at her for skipping dinner with Deke only to wind up at the pub with Riley. She and Deke didn't have anything officially personal beyond their weekly coffee, yet she sensed he wanted something more from her. Something more that she'd thought she was interested in, as well, despite her reluctance to cross that line.

Well, she thought as her cheeks heated, she'd certainly leaped over that line with both lips and most of her body last night with Riley. Which meant it was time to clear the air with Deke. Hopefully, she was just misinterpreting his signals. Braced for embarrassment, she tried to explain.

She cleared her throat. "I was close to the station, though I didn't intend to be. After I called you, I came home to find my neighbors had been decorating like crazy. My yard looked stark in comparison." She couldn't stop babbling. "One of my neighbors helped me get caught up in record time. The least I could do was buy him a burger at the pub."

"Of course. Your passion for this community is what makes you stand out. It's what makes them love you so," Deke said, waving off her concern with a flick of his hand. "Think nothing of it, my dear. Our plans were tentative at best. I only came out today to see a friend and offer a bit of encouragement during this ordeal."

Ordeal felt a little strong, but Deke enjoyed formality and drama. It showed in his work as well as every other facet of his life, including impersonating a floral delivery driver. And she wasn't about to quibble over semantics with a friend.

"Thank you. The flowers are gorgeous and definitely brightened my day."

His gaze roamed around the room and she was afraid to ask what he thought. Compared to the grand expanse of his home, hers must be a laughable disappointment. But none of those reactions showed on his face.

"I heard you had a little trouble yourself."

"Someone broke into my garage and tried to tie me to a murder."

"That's absurd. Do you need a lawyer?"

She was sure he could afford the best. "No. I cleared it up with the Baltimore P.D. first thing this morning. While no one knows how my shovel got involved, it wasn't the murder weapon."

"What a relief. For all of us." His smile was kind and friendly as he pushed to his feet and donned the ball cap and gloves. "Tomorrow's opening day will be a resounding success," he declared. "I'm sure of it." He gave her a quick hug. "And the city will have you to thank."

"Not just me," she said, uncomfortable with his effusive praise. "Everyone has worked together to make this the best season ever. Thanks for everything, Deke."

"It's my pleasure."

She locked the door when he returned to his car. On her way back to the kitchen she paused to enjoy the flowers. It was a thoughtful gesture, a bit over the top, but thoughtful. The arrangement was too big for her small kitchen table, but she felt too exposed working in the front room.

If this was her worst dilemma today, things were looking up.

Chapter Eleven

Home from his errand, Deke tapped an impatient rhythm on the cold pane of the window. He was surrounded by idiots. The man on the ladder hadn't had the decency to die. Somehow no one had put Chief Jensen into cuffs for bashing a repeat offender over the head with her shovel, despite her lack of a believable alibi. And now, rather than inciting fear, the fire had seemingly fueled the woman's determination to maintain her hard stance against the attacks on her town.

He cursed the skills that had put him in this precarious position. It wasn't his job to micromanage something as pedestrian as the crime-versus-law balance in Belclare and yet those who kept him in business insisted he clean it up. Fools. They were wasting his talent.

His job was creating the strategies that furthered the cause. Tempted to ignore his orders in favor of more effective strikes elsewhere, he soothed himself with the small progress he'd made with the police chief.

The only other consolation was that revenue from the Christmas Village would surely be down in light of the current violence. No amount of greenery and twinkling lights could hide the stain on Belclare, and the shopkeepers who needed the financial infusion would force their once-beloved chief of police out of the way long enough for him to take a giant leap forward in making reparations.

The latest drug shipment was half the size of the one Abby had discovered. Thanks to the distraction of the fire, it had come and gone already with no one the wiser. Now, with his superiors slightly at ease, he could focus on vengeance. He picked up the phone and relayed his next orders.

Waiting for the fun to start, he contemplated all the ways things could go right. And wrong.

If he couldn't bring Chief Jensen to him with the promise of a friendship, he could certainly prey on her need to defend and protect. Either way, he would be thrilled when she finally came running right into his trap.

Her new neighbor was no match for Deke. If he got in the way he would be just another casualty of this war.

Chapter Twelve

Riley spent the morning much as he'd spent the night: thinking of Abby. Not just the kiss, but the serious threat chasing her around town. Personally and professionally, the woman and her predicament consumed his attention.

His arms full of plastic wrapping and cardboard boxes, he headed out to the Dumpsters and recycling bins. He pulled out his knife and sliced through the tape, breaking down the boxes for recycling. The decorating team was nearly done setting up and not a moment too soon. A light snow was predicted for this evening, which would surely make tomorrow's opening day perfect for all the expected visitors.

As he walked back into the warehouse, he spotted a black wallet caught between the Dumpster and the warehouse. He pulled out the tri-folded leather, only to realize it was a woman's wallet. Looking around, he didn't see any of the women who were part of the crew. Figuring someone would come forward soon, he walked on into the supervisor's office. "Anyone looking for this?" he asked, holding it up.

His boss removed his reading glasses. "No one's said anything to me."

"I found it behind the Dumpster and thought I'd rather have a witness when I open it."

His boss nodded. "Go for it. Then I need you to make sure the welcome sign is done right."

With a nod, Riley popped the snap and stared, dumbfounded by the image of Mrs. Wilks on the driver's license. "What the hell?"

"You know her?"

"She lives down the street from the house I'm renting."

His boss checked the clock on the wall. "Take it over to her, grab some lunch then swing by and check on the welcome sign. The pair on that is more likely to build a snowman than finish the job in a timely manner."

"Sure thing."

Fifteen minutes later, Riley was across town and parked in his driveway next to Abby's car. After the fire he knew she'd be working from home and he had to squash the urge to knock on her door just to say hello.

If he played his cards right, maybe he could get a repeat performance of last night's kisses. Which was not exactly why Director Casey had planted him here. Denying himself the satisfaction of admiring the work they'd done on her yard, he fixed his attention forward and kept on walking down the sidewalk.

"Riley?"

Abby.

He turned back to greet her. "Hey." She was dressed in a sweater and jeans. He had yet to decide which wardrobe he preferred, the professional one or her more casual side. She looked so temping in everything she wore.

"Are you already done for the day?"

He wanted to believe that was hope he heard in her voice. "No." He held up the wallet.

"What's that?"

"Mrs. Wilks's wallet. I'm returning it."

It didn't matter that he was on the sidewalk and she was

standing in her doorway—he could see doubt stamped all over her face.

"Where did you find it?" She stepped outside and pulled her door closed behind her.

"Near the Dumpster behind the warehouse."

"When?"

He looked at his watch. "About an hour ago."

"And you walked all the way over here."

"No." He pointed to his truck. "It's my lunch break. I drove over here to return it. I'm guessing she doesn't realize she lost it. Or that someone nabbed it."

"Do you not hear how odd that sounds?"

"Maybe," he admitted. "Are you accusing me of something?"

She hesitated, then shook her head. "No." She came down the walk to join him. "Can I take a look?"

"If you'd rather be the one to give it back to her, be my guest." Irritated with the way she twisted him up, he handed the wallet over and started back for his house.

"Hang on." She reached out and caught him lightly at the waist. The heat and strength of her fingers startled him almost as much as the sizzle that shot through his system at the contact. After last night, he should have expected it. "I don't mean to be overprotective of the people I care about."

He nodded. "It's probably habit by now."

"Even if she wasn't a friend," Abby said, "her safety is my responsibility."

He covered her hands with his. "I understand. You take it over and I'll head back to work." He wasn't sure what to do next. He wanted to kiss her but knew she'd rather not have anyone on the street see that kind of display. And he didn't trust his control around her. When she didn't move, he frowned. "What's wrong? You look upset." Had something else happened?

"I'm not upset."

Her pale face and rapid breath offered a decent imper-sonation of pretty-damn-scared, but he took the safe route and didn't share his thoughts. "I get it. She matters to you. This worries you. Go." He jerked his head toward the street. "Make sure she's okay."

"It's just that…" Abby cleared her throat, but she wouldn't meet his gaze. "Lately I…imagine the worst in every situation. Come on, let's take it to her together."

Her admission showed him just how far they'd come so very quickly. She trusted him to some degree. That meant a great deal to him on more levels than one.

When they reached Mrs. Wilks's door, Abby pressed the doorbell and they listened to the happy chime beyond the closed door. Once the familiar tune had faded, silence filled the air.

Several seconds passed then Riley asked, "Does she nap in the afternoons?"

"She's too busy to nap," Abby said, turning to walk around to the back of the house.

"Then she's out. Without her wallet," he observed. "Her car's not in the driveway."

Ignoring him, Abby knocked at the back door and called out. When no one answered, she tried the knob, but even with a little jiggle, it remained locked.

"Turn around," she said. "I know where she keeps a key."

Trying not to laugh, he did as ordered while she retrieved the spare key. She probably didn't want to know that he'd already identified the hiding place under the second step near the handrail. It was the cleanest spot on the stairs.

Hadn't he just decided that Abby was beginning to trust him? *Ha!*

"All right." Abby reached for the door. "Let's go in and check on her."

They really didn't have any evidence that something was wrong. Except the wallet in his hand. He didn't know her well, but Mrs. Wilks didn't strike him as the sort to toss her wallet out by mistake. Not to mention he couldn't imagine what business she had at the docks. The same things were probably running through Abby's mind.

"Mrs. Wilks?" Abby's voice carried through the kitchen.

As Riley followed her inside, he noticed the only light came from the window over the sink and the door they'd opened. The coffeepot on the counter was full, but the warmer light was off. A programmable model, he realized as Abby called out again. He tried not to jump to conclusions, but this wasn't adding up to anything good.

"Does she have family nearby?"

"Her son lives in Baltimore," Abby answered. "Mrs. Wilks? It's Abby and—crap."

Abby had flipped on the hallway light. Crap didn't begin to define the mess. From his position behind her he could see the overturned umbrella stand, smashed pictures of grandchildren and other bits and pieces of Mrs. Wilks's decor broken and scattered across the floor.

Clearly, whoever had broken into her house wasn't worried about leaving a mess. A rush through the house confirmed Mrs. Wilks was not at home.

Abby turned on him. "When was the last time you saw her?"

He studied her, recognized her cop persona. "Is this another interrogation?"

"No. Maybe." She clenched her fists. "Just answer me. I need a time frame."

He thought about it. "I haven't seen her since Calder got hurt."

Abby's shoulders slumped. "Damn it. I was afraid you'd say that. She didn't help with the decorating yesterday?"

He shook his head. "When did you see her last?"

Her lips quivered. "I checked with her yesterday morning after discovering the damaged lock on my garage, but she said she didn't hear anything." She shook her head. "How did I go an entire day and not miss her?"

Riley could rattle off the reasons but figured it would only add to her misplaced guilt. "We can ask around the block, see if anyone saw anything."

"That's a good idea." She held out her hand for the wallet. "I'll hang on to this and call in someone to start a report and a search for her car."

Riley wanted to hold her and give her some comfort but knew she'd resist. She'd switched over to police chief mode and all he could do was try to help.

He'd seen her face when Calder had been hurt, when the station was on fire, and thought he knew her pained expression. Neither incident had anything on the torment haunting her vivid blue eyes right now. She blamed herself and he didn't have the words to reassure her.

"I'm sorry I pulled it away from the Dumpster." He wanted to take some of the burden, but she didn't let it go.

Abby caught her lower lip between her teeth. "I doubt that will make any difference. I'll send a team over there to look around just in case."

He heard her muttering oaths and violent promises as she called for backup. By the time he exited the back door, two of Belclare's finest were emerging from cruisers, guns drawn.

"Hold it right there."

Riley stopped, raised his hands. "Take it easy, officers. Chief Jensen is inside."

"What have you done with her?"

"Abby," he called over his shoulder.

"No," snapped the officer closest to the steps. "What have you done with Mrs. Wilks?"

"I haven't done anything with her."

"Riley?" Abby walked out the side door. She swore when she saw her officers. "Gadsden, what's going on?"

He wished her first request had been for them to lower their weapons, but he could wait it out. He hoped.

"We found Mrs. Wilks's car down by the docks. Evidence inside the vehicle led us to the Hamilton place. There we found a scarf belonging to Mrs. Wilks on the rail by the back door. Since that's where O'Brien is living, makes sense that he knows something about her sudden disappearance."

"Riley?"

He hated the doubt he heard in Abby's voice. More, he hated the person orchestrating this mess. Riley had already vetted everyone on the Belclare police force and come up empty. He'd yet to find anyone who had a beef with Calder, which confirmed his suspicion that someone was using the community to torture Abby. It wasn't a stretch to see the deadly potential here and Riley had to find a way to head it off.

"I found a scarf last night when I got home," Riley said, his eyes still on the weapons aimed at him. "It was caught in the door, so I picked it up, looped it over the rail," he explained. "I don't have a clue where it came from."

"You need to come with us, Mr. O'Brien."

"Wait a second," Abby said in her no-nonsense chief's voice. "Put away your weapons."

Finally. Riley lowered his hands but kept them in plain view. "Thanks," he murmured to her as the officers complied.

"What evidence led you to Riley's—the Hamilton house?"

"A tool with O'Brien's name on it. Everyone in town knows he moved in there."

"Never tried to hide it," Riley tossed out.

"Hush," Abby said. "What kind of tool?"

Gadsden clearly preferred that Riley implicate himself, but he relented. "A hammer."

With a tight nod, Riley silently vowed that he'd get even with the bastard behind this. "I haven't kidnapped anyone. I have at least three hammers in the truck. There's always one on my tool belt. I used one yesterday when we set up the park display and again when we decorated the street. You can check with my coworkers or any of the neighbors."

"We'll need to check your story. Let's take a walk," Gadsden suggested. "I have a few more questions for you."

"No." Abby denied that request. "Do you have any sort of timeline yet?"

"The dock workers who reported the car don't recall seeing it parked out there before this morning."

"So you're thinking this all happened last night."

Gadsden nodded. "It's possible the fire was a diversion."

"I'm starting to agree," Abby said, giving voice to one of Riley's developing theories.

He could not afford to waste time in a holding cell. He didn't think she could afford to be without his protection, even though she didn't realize that was his real purpose here. Once more he toyed with the idea of telling her the truth, but he wasn't about to admit anything in front of her officers.

"I found the scarf when I came home for the night." He just managed to avoid Abby's gaze. "Around eleven."

"Did you see him arrive home, Chief?"

"Yes." She gestured to the door she'd exited. "We have a crime scene inside that needs to be processed. From what I can see—the bed hasn't been slept in and the coffee that brewed automatically this morning is still waiting in the carafe—Mrs. Wilks was attacked and taken from her home late last night."

"You didn't see anyone hanging around before that?" Gadsden pressed.

"No," Abby said resolutely.

Riley kept studying the policemen. Between the crowd at the pub and the bystanders at the fire, surely they'd heard he'd driven Abby home. What were they tiptoeing around?

"We'd like to take him in for questioning."

"No," Abby repeated. "He was with me," she said with a resigned sigh. "I drove home from the station and Riley met me out front to help me decorate my house. Before that, Danny and Peg can vouch for his contribution to decorating the rest of the street."

"Yes, ma'am. But after that?"

"After, I took Mr. O'Brien to the pub for dinner. It was a dinner we never finished because Martin Filmore went off the deep end and set our police station on fire."

Gadsden rocked back on his heels. "And after that?"

In Gadsden's place, Riley would've ducked from the laser glare Abby aimed at him. "I watched him walk over to his house."

"Did you watch him go inside?"

"No."

"So you can't verify his story about the scarf."

"I can verify everything else, including his character, Officer Gadsden," she said pointedly.

Riley muted his shock over that statement. She must trust him more than he thought. Well, she had kissed him first. And she'd let him keep kissing her once he'd recovered from the unexpected surprise.

"Yes, ma'am." Gadsden rubbed his palm over his holstered weapon. "But why frame him?"

"Good question," she countered. "Why don't you start figuring it out?"

Riley gave the officer credit for persistence.

"Based on the evidence of a struggle inside and everything you've found we need to assume the worst," Abby relented. "But Riley was not involved in her disappearance."

"All right." Gadsden acquiesced.

"Give me the address for the car," Abby instructed. "I'll head that way. You two can take over here."

"Yes, ma'am."

"Come on," she said to Riley. "We'll take my car. Give them your keys."

He raised his eyebrows but pulled them out of his pocket.

"When you're done with this scene, process his truck. Thoroughly," she instructed. "I'll make sure his prints get into the system so you can rule them out."

He told himself the cover story established by the Specialists would hold up under the scrutiny of the Belclare police department and he fell into step beside her. She darted into her house, returned seconds later with her purse and then rushed for her car.

"How are they going to process anything without a police station?"

Abby unclipped her keys from her purse strap. "Filmore was kind enough to leave us with half of a police station."

"Just not the half your office was in."

"Exactly." She nodded, pulling open her car door. "We're wasting time. Get in."

She barely waited for him to buckle his seat belt before she hit the sirens and went barreling out of the neighborhood.

"You're angry," he observed.

Abby thought about that as she negotiated the light traffic. Moving to a smaller town was the best thing she'd ever done. For herself and her career. She wasn't going to let some sick bastard ruin that by picking off her friends. "Yes."

"About being my alibi?"

"Only a little," she admitted.

"Your officers are protective and loyal. That's a good thing."

He had a valid point, which only emphasized how any of the men and women on the Belclare force could become targets at any time. Had, in fact, if she considered last night's fire.

She slowed for the congestion on Main Street and it gave her time to glance at him. In profile his face was stern, his eyes on the road. The clean-shaved jaw was set with a determination that mirrored hers. He'd been so calm and steady with Calder and again at the fire. He'd barely flinched when Gadsden and Miller had been ready to haul him in. Somehow it made her feel better about taking a civilian to another crime scene. For the briefest of seconds, she wondered again if she was a fool to let him so close. She'd certainly misread Filmore, but she couldn't dwell on that mistake.

"I'm angry that some maladjusted perp is yanking me around and messing with my friends." She stomped on the accelerator once she was clear of the traffic. "More than that, I'm worried about Mrs. Wilks."

"We'll find her."

"We damn well better find her alive. If he's killed her—"

"He?"

She focused on the road. At this speed she had to or she'd be risking their lives, too. And she wasn't letting the person responsible for all of this off that easily. "A generic term at this point."

"But?"

How did he know there was a "but"? She supposed it

was obvious. "Some of the more recent emails, the more personal threats, feel like they've been written by one person. Male. Thanks to technology they might be coming in from all across the globe, but I think one man is leading this vendetta against me."

"That's a big leap, Abby. The video was a smash hit."

She swore, taking the fork toward the docks. "It's Chief Jensen when we're on scene."

"Yes, ma'am."

He sounded like Gadsden. She didn't have time to decide how she felt about that. As they approached the scene, she left her lights on but turned off the siren. "I know you didn't do this. When we get there feel free to verify that's your hammer."

"Unless it isn't."

"Unless it isn't," she echoed. She couldn't picture Riley kidnapping Mrs. Wilks with a hammer or anything else. Maybe he'd hold her hostage for more cookies. The idea made her want to smile. But first she had to find her neighbor…and friend.

She parked the car and prepared herself for the worst. If Mrs. Wilks had been found, they would've radioed that information to her en route.

"Chief Jensen."

"Yes?" She faced Riley, startled by the intensity in his golden brown eyes.

"I *didn't* do this."

"I know." Her instincts wouldn't be that skewed by a few hot kisses and helpful deeds. Looking away from him, she let her gaze wander across the docks. A time-worn industrial scene on the best of days, the mismatched collection of warehouses, cranes and container yard weren't any more inviting with the dusting of snow.

"We have to find her," she said to herself. "I won't let

some faceless terrorists win." She exited the car, grateful she'd opted for sturdy denim trousers and a thick sweater for working at home today.

The grim expressions on the responding officers' faces told her they hadn't come up with anything positive, but she asked for the status anyway.

"Nothing new." Detective Calloway slid a dark look toward Riley. "What's he doing here?"

She found it interesting that Gadsden hadn't called ahead with a warning that Riley was with her. "He's not responsible for this," she said in an unyielding tone. "He can also verify if the item that implicates him is in fact his."

Calloway scowled at Riley. "Come on then. It's over here."

She watched every nuance of Riley's body language for stress and found none. He was either very good at hiding his reactions, or absolutely oblivious to the risks. Despite her belief in his innocence, they had to follow the evidence.

The detective held the hammer, enveloped in an evidence bag, in front of Riley's face. "It has your name on it, O'Brien."

Abby continued to watch for an indicator that Riley was lying about any of this. He didn't even flinch as he manipulated the hammer inside the bag until his name showed. "Every temp worker in town has used one like this at some point this week. It's company issue." He handed it back. "Name or not, that isn't mine."

He didn't need to start lying now. "Your name is right there on the handle," she argued.

"Sure is," he agreed. "But that isn't how I write my name."

"What?" She and the detective took a closer look at the same time.

"Compare it to the tools in my truck and you'll see. Someone else wrote my name there."

She nodded at Calloway. He called over to Gadsden for a quick picture and count of the hammers in Riley's truck. When the picture proved Riley was correct, she sighed, relieved and frustrated. She appreciated the confirmation of his innocence, but they weren't any closer to finding Mrs. Wilks.

"What now?" Calloway wanted to know.

"We talk to the folks who reported the abandoned vehicle."

With a nod to Riley, she invited him to tag along as she posed her questions to the workers on-site. No one had been spotted coming or going from the vehicle. There were a few cameras on the docks, which had helped her bust the drug runners, but Mrs. Wilks's car had been placed in a blind spot.

"On purpose," Riley observed as they walked around the area. "They did a sloppy job trying to frame me," he added.

She looked down the docks. The company he worked for was renting space in the warehouse farthest from the water. It was the largest but also offered better security and more parking. "What are the cameras like at your warehouse?"

"Are you kidding?" Riley pushed his hands into his pockets. "With all the negative attention, the boss added his own closed-circuit system. Says it's the first time he felt like he had to."

"Does everyone on the team know that?"

Riley shrugged. "I think so, but can't say for sure."

She walked back to where Calloway was overseeing the arrival of the tow truck for Mrs. Wilks's car. "Let's get the video from the warehouse where Riley works. Maybe we'll identify who tossed the wallet at the Dumpster."

Calloway hustled off to do as she requested. The only

thing left to do was examine the car and she wanted to get that done before it was towed to the impound lot. Abby's gut twisted, but she couldn't avoid the inevitable. She told herself the odds of finding anything her officers had over-looked were slim to none, but she had to try. She owed it to her neighbor.

"Come on," she said to Riley, handing him latex gloves. She had no desire to do this alone. Let the department— hell, the entire town—speculate, but she needed his sup-port right now on a very personal level.

Mrs. Wilks was more than a neighbor, she'd become a dear friend. Based on the latest trash in Abby's in-box, the man tormenting her had targeted and kidnapped Mrs. Wilks solely because she and Abby were friends. With every step, the burdens got heavier. The symbolic vandal-ism. Calder. Her shovel used against one of the vandals. Filmore and the fire.

She paused at the driver's side, gazing across the top of the car at Riley. "I'm done playing catch-up here. We find Mrs. Wilks and then I'm doing whatever it takes to put this to rest."

"Sounds like a plan."

Abby didn't quite know how she'd do it, but she knew it was past time. There had to be some way to connect the dots and put a stop to this. Belclare was her town and she wouldn't cower in a corner while terrorists dealt out fear. She put on the gloves to preserve any evidence and opened the driver's door.

The driver's seat was pushed back much too far for Mrs. Wilks's smaller frame. "She didn't drive herself," she noted.

"Which might mean two perps. One to drive, one to control the hostage."

Abby nodded, bending down for a closer look at the

floor mats. "She's feisty. It might have required two perps just to subdue her."

"When does she prepare her coffeemaker?"

"Huh?"

"She has a programmable pot. It was full and turned off when we were in the house. She had to have set it at some point."

"Typically, she does that during the commercial break before the news. At least, that's what I've seen her do on the rare occasions I was there at that time of night."

"All right. Neither of us saw any strange cars on the street when we got home from the fire."

Abby's face heated as she recalled those steamy kisses. "We weren't exactly looking for anything out of place."

He shot her a wicked grin, the one full of sexy promises that made her pulse kick in hopeful anticipation. She ruthlessly reminded herself they were at a crime scene.

"Look at that." He pointed to the floor cushion in the backseat closest to her side.

She opened the back door and shifted, letting the bright sunlight fall on a pink smudge on the upholstery. She sniffed at it, recognizing the cosmetic fragrance. "Lipstick. Damn it."

Abby stood up, pulling the crisp air deep into her lungs, willing her stomach to settle down.

"Well, it's confirmation she or someone wearing lipstick was in the car," Riley said, coming over to her side so they could speak without being overheard. "Unless she typically kissed her backseat."

She opened her mouth to say they'd known that already, but he was right—without an eyewitness, they'd been assuming Mrs. Wilks had been a passenger in the car.

"Okay." Abby took another deep breath. "You and I arrived in the neighborhood just after eleven. Mrs. Wilks would have made her coffee before that. Assuming the altercation was limited to the hallway, one or two men grabbed her from her house before the evening news wrapped up.

Abby might have heard something if she hadn't been in the shower wishing she had the guts to invite Riley over to wash her back. A weak laugh slipped out at the thought. If she'd done that, bringing him out of his house, he might actually have seen or heard something.

"This isn't your fault, Chief Jensen," he said.

She cursed herself for allowing him to see the uncertainties nagging at her. "Not quite what I was thinking, but close enough." She pointed to the tires. "I'm not seeing anything on the tread or wheel wells that I wouldn't expect to find in Belclare."

"So what did they do in between grabbing her and dumping the car?"

Refusing to let her emotions run amok down that path, Abby regained a small measure of control. Planting her hands on her hips, she said, "Let's check the trunk."

"No one's done that?"

"They said it was empty, but I want to look anyway."

"Fresh eyes?"

"Exactly." She went around to the passenger side and popped open the glove box to hit the trunk release. The car shifted when the trunk lid opened. "There has to be some clue about what they've done with her."

"Stop." Riley held up a hand, his gaze locked on the interior of the trunk.

"What?"

"Back away and pull back the others, too."

"Tell me why," she insisted.

"Bomb."

The single word, delivered so calmly, jolted her system.

"The trunk was empty when they found the car. No one could have planted a bomb since my guys got here."

"Abby," he warned. "Listen to me. Please."

What could he possibly know about bombs? But his face was pale and now his body was rigid with tension. "I'm not leaving without taking a look."

He shook his head, sending her a ferocious scowl, but she didn't care. He had to be wrong. Her people had already popped the trunk and declared it empty and void of evidence.

"Fine. But call in a bomb squad while you look."

Belclare didn't have a bomb squad. She couldn't recall for sure, but one of the firefighters might have had military experience with disarming explosives. The closest fully trained team was in Baltimore. "Is there a timer?"

"I don't know yet."

She stepped up next to him, but all she saw was the coarse fabric lining the trunk. "Riley, what am I missing here?"

"Too many wires into the brake lights." He pointed out the difference between the right and left sides. "Call someone, *now*."

"There's no one local," she whispered, even as she entered the number for the state police. "If we're lucky they can have someone here in half an hour." *Lucky* being the operative word.

No sooner had she'd ended the call than the sound of heavy engines jerked her attention to the parking lot behind them. She swore when two media vans stopped at the perimeter, as she'd requested. "Great. Now we'll have an audience."

"Someone tipped them off."

"Possibly, but anyone can listen to the police radio," she replied, equally irritated. "Tell me what to do."

"Any chance you'll back off while I take a closer look?"

"No."

She watched as he looked around the docks.

"You felt the car shift when you hit the button, right?"

"Yes." She'd definitely felt it.

"I'm going to look for some kind of timer."

She held her breath when he leaned into the trunk, pulling a knife from his pocket. She appreciated his concern, but if the terrorists wanted her dead, they could detonate the bomb at any time—an assessment that assumed they were watching this play out.

Riley's back blocked her view, so she used her cell to update the officers behind them. There was no way to be subtle about clearing the area, especially when she didn't know how big a threat they were dealing with.

Finally, she couldn't take it anymore. "Riley?"

"It's counting down, Abby. Please get to safety."

Fear trickled into her veins. "Only if you're coming with me."

"I'll be right behind you."

"I don't believe you." She actually laughed a little when he swore. "Can you disarm it?"

"Not sure," he said.

Every second seemed to tick by with individual clarity. "How much time?"

"Enough."

"Good."

"No. Weird. Ask yourself who benefits from blowing this up while you stand by helplessly?"

She cast a glance over her shoulder at the media. "I know who it hurts. All of Belclare. Is there anything resembling evidence?"

"Probably, but the explosion will destroy it," he countered. "Get me the keys."

"Why?"

"Do it, Chief Jensen. The sooner this is resolved, the sooner we can find Mrs. Wilks."

She darted back to Calloway. He found the right evidence bag and tossed it to her. But when she turned back, she realized Riley had tricked her into leaving him.

Somehow he'd started the car without the key and was steering Mrs. Wilks sedan toward the water.

Understanding dawned slowly. He intended to put the car in the water to save the surrounding area from the explosion. What had he seen on that bomb and why hadn't he been honest about it? For that matter, why didn't the terrorists behind this throw the switch? She didn't want Riley in any more danger, but the tactics didn't make sense. None of this made sense.

His words echoed in her mind and she prayed they weren't the last ones she'd hear him speak. *Who gains?* The phrase consumed her as she alternately watched the sedan's progress and the people gathered around watching with her. Any one of them could have a thumb on a detonator ready to make this a spectacular tragedy.

Who gains? She couldn't come up with an answer, not while she watched a civilian, a stranger who'd so quickly slipped through her defenses, sacrifice himself. If he lived, she might have to beat him senseless for putting her through this.

The sedan's engine revved suddenly and she waited for the explosion, but Riley jumped out of the driver's seat and the car rolled off the dock and into the water.

Riley hadn't even gained his feet when the explosion sent water spouting into the air like a fountain.

Heedless of the media and public opinion, she raced down the dock to check on him. "What the hell were you thinking?" she shouted in his face even as she looked him up and down.

"I'm fine, thanks for asking."

"That was stupid."

"Would you rather the thing blew up the dock? Imagine the fallout. The lost revenue. The cleanup."

"Stop using logic. You could've been killed."

"I don't think so."

"What does that mean?" She wanted to hug him and punch him at the same time. "I should have you arrested."

"On what grounds?"

"You're a danger to yourself."

"But not to others?"

She didn't have time to dignify that. They'd reached the area where the police had been holding people back and everyone burst into applause and cheers.

"Smile," she instructed, although she knew he was already doing so. "You're a hero."

"An hour ago I was a suspect."

"Not in my book," she said.

She answered a few questions posed by the reporters of the local station and let Mayor Scott, who'd caught the scent of a good public relations opportunity, handle the rest. Once she'd given instructions to the officers on the scene, she pulled Riley away from the noise and chaos.

"Even with the bomb neutralized, it will be a wonder if anyone comes out tomorrow," she grumbled.

"It will probably be the biggest opening day ever."

"That's not funny," she said. "We still have to find Mrs. Wilks."

"I have an idea, but you're not going to like it."

"Try me. She's my number-one priority." Once she found her neighbor, then Abby would take the time to ask how Riley had developed such a thorough recognition of bombs.

She was sure there was a reasonable explanation, but she wanted to hear it from him.

The Belclare police force wasn't comprised of idiots, but they hadn't noticed the threat when they'd searched the trunk. Unless one of them was in on it.

She jerked herself back from that slippery slope. Paranoia would not resolve this any sooner for her lost neighbor.

"Here." Riley handed her a rolled-up piece of paper.

"What's this?" She opened it, startled to see a line sketch of the Belclare shore. Three different points were marked with different numbers.

"It was wrapped around the primary wire."

"Dear Lord," she whispered. "That's why they left her car out here. It's a countdown game."

He nodded. "One sick scavenger hunt. If it's counting from the explosion in the car, that only gives us ten more minutes to reach the first point."

"She won't be at that one."

"You can't be sure," he said gently. "And someone else might be."

He was right. Her stomach pitched and rolled. Anger and fear fought for dominance, but neither would help save Mrs. Wilks or anyone else.

"She's an innocent old lady," Abby said through clenched teeth. It infuriated her that people she cared about were suffering because she knew how to do her job. Because she'd vowed to keep Belclare crime-free. "She might already be dead of exposure."

Riley rubbed her arms, chasing away the chill that threatened to drag her under. "You have to stay positive."

Positive was becoming exhausting. "But be prepared for the worst."

He acknowledged her comment with a bob of his head. "I can get started while you organize a search party."

"No. This is personal and I'm done taking risks with the lives of those who trust me."

"Abby, if you ditch protocol and rules now, every effort you've made is for nothing. Stick with your system. It works."

He was right and Mrs. Wilks needed Abby at the top of her game.

"I'm heading to the first point. Get a team together and do this the right way."

"Fine. I'll be right behind you," she said, echoing his words from earlier.

"I believe you," he said, smiling.

She longed to give him a kiss, but that would make him more of a target than he already was.

As she shared the map with Calloway and issued orders, pairing off available troops in different directions, her mind mulled over the question of *who gains*.

Today's events only confirmed her worst suspicions. This wasn't simply a matter of random thugs descending on her town to prove a point. No, the problems were being meticulously planned and carried out from right inside Belclare.

The feds had warned her that the drugs might be funding a sleeper cell. But she hadn't wanted to believe anyone in her town was capable of fooling the entire community that way. She hadn't wanted to admit she'd been fooled.

By their nature sleeper cells blended in, participated and carried on as valuable members of a community. Until called to action.

The drug bust had not been a random event. The vandals, Calder's attacker, Filmore. Mrs. Wilks's kidnapper. The evidence planted to implicate both her and Riley in different crimes. None of it had been random.

As the search teams set off, Abby jogged along in Riley's wake. She wasn't about to let her newest ally face her enemies alone.

Chapter Thirteen

Riley didn't hold out much hope that Mrs. Wilks would be at the first marker as he rushed down to the rocky shoreline. That would be too easy. He pulled his cell phone from his pocket, checked the reception and entered Director Casey's personal number.

"This is unexpected," Casey answered.

"Yes, sir. Things are escalating rapidly. Do you have anything connecting the names I sent?"

"Not yet."

Riley paused, picking his way around an outcropping of sharp slate-colored stones. "Calder is clean." He'd thought Calder's accident might have been staged to disguise his link to the terrorist cell, but not anymore. The man had no ties to the drug runners and while Calder knew Filmore, their association had been strictly professional. "It's like ghosts taking potshots around here."

"Stay on it," Casey said. "Belclare needs you. We picked up the call to the state police for backup. FYI, they have a bomb squad but it likely won't arrive in time."

On that sour news the call ended. Riley put his phone away and checked his watch. He had to be getting close to the first marker.

He looked over his shoulder at the docks. The search teams Abby had put into play were combing other parts of the shoreline. Riley gazed out across the water. One of the tugboats was motoring out into the bay. Hopefully the team on board was working for their side and not the terrorists. Checking his watch, he had less than three minutes to find the marker or, if the map and timing were accurate, there would be another explosion.

"Mrs. Wilks!" he called out, praying there wasn't another victim to rescue...or recover.

He chose his steps with more care, alert for a glimpse of a trip wire or any sign someone had been here. He saw it then, a rounded cache of stones that wasn't quite as natural as the rest of the area. He approached with extreme caution despite the dwindling time, unwilling to rush and set something off prematurely.

A bullet whistled past his head, knocking the top stone from the cache. Riley had jerked back, seeking cover, when he heard the soft whimper.

"Mrs. Wilks?"

Another muffled response came from closer to the scruffy, wind-sculpted trees to his left. Rocks and twigs skittered down the slope toward him.

He took that as an affirmative.

The small cascade revealed red and green wires running from the cache of rocks up into the trees. Definitely a bomb, he thought grimly. "Hold still," he called out to the woman. God help them both if she did something to set it off.

He peered up but couldn't pick out the armed guard. The shooter could be anywhere, in a tree or undercover on the ground.

In the back of his mind, a clock seemed to tick off the seconds. He wondered about the twisted strategist who'd gone to such lengths just to get even with Abby. Whatever the goal, he had to deal with this first.

Stretched out on his belly, he inched closer to the wiring. Another bullet bit into the rock-strewn ground milli-meters from his fingertips. Splintered rocks bit at his face. Even if he'd had a weapon it wouldn't have done him much good at the moment. There was no time for him to stop and return fire.

Both he and the guard were equally determined to suc-ceed, with Mrs. Wilks's life in the balance. Riley shifted as fast as he dared up the slope and the radio at his belt crackled.

"At your back," Abby's voice came through the device.

Despite his precarious position, Riley smiled. Of course she had his back. Thinking about how the bomb in the car had been wired, he went for the cache of explosives closer to the water. He couldn't afford to waste precious seconds with a panicked hostage.

This time when the sniper fired, another weapon re-turned fire. Out of habit, Riley kept track of the bullets from Abby. The Belclare P.D. used 9mm handguns with a fifteen-round clip. Whatever Abby was firing was beefier than that, the sound too deep for a standard 9mm.

His attention on the bomb, he ignored the shouting, knowing Abby would follow protocol and ask for a sur-render. The timer was inside twenty seconds when Riley disconnected the detonator. He followed the wires up the bank, another volley of gunfire flying over his head.

"Mrs. Wilks!" Relief at finding her alive washed over him and he wanted to shout in victory when he saw the timer on the device strapped to her waist frozen at twelve seconds. "You're fine. It's over," he said, cutting through the tape and sliding the explosives away from her.

Her round face was pale under the dirt and her eyes were shining with tears. "This might hurt," he warned, gently peeling away the duct tape covering her mouth. He looked at the adhesive side, noting the smudge of pink lipstick.

"Thank you!" She threw herself into him and he caught her, letting her cling.

"Are you hurt?"

"My pride," she said, tears flowing freely now. "The bruises will heal faster, I'm sure, but I'm so cold."

"Nothing broken?" He pulled the radio from his belt and called for paramedics. "Nothing bleeding?"

"I'm fine," she insisted. "My word. They were shooting at you."

He decided the woman had an ironclad fortitude to be more worried about him than herself. "It wasn't as close as it looked. Did you see who did this to you? Can you give us a description?" Then he noticed something missing. "You aren't wearing your glasses."

"Young man, my distance vision is still perfect."

Which meant she might or might not be able to describe the person or persons who had done this to her.

Tree limbs popped and snapped as something crashed down nearly on top of them.

"Get down!" He didn't hesitate at Abby's command, pushing Mrs. Wilks back into the shallow hollow that might well have been her grave.

He heard one more deep shot from Abby's gun, followed by a terrible sound that split the air in two. The concussion wave from the explosion threw him down and a blast of heat kept him there while pieces of trees and rock and ash fell all around them like dirty rain.

Two more loud explosions sounded too close for comfort, shaking the earth and rocks under them. It reminded him of the day he'd watched a crew take down an old building two blocks from the orphanage. He hoped that meant the other caches were blown and this trial was over.

The eerie silence that followed swallowed him up, surrounding him and Mrs. Wilks. He peered out at the shore and spotted the grisly debris of what had surely been the sniper.

"Where is Abby?" Mrs. Wilks cried. "Is she all right?"

Riley twisted around to check the place he'd last heard her, smiling when she stood tall, leaning into the slope, her gun down and just behind her leg. "I'm right here, Mrs. Wilks," she called out. Her chest heaved as she gulped in air. "Don't worry about me."

Riley moved a bit so the older woman could see her friend and neighbor.

"Oh, thank heaven. Thank heaven for both of you." She clasped her hands over her heart, then let Riley help her to her feet. He kept her turned from the mess closer to the shore as Abby stepped forward to wrap her in a warm hug. "Help will be here shortly. You don't have to walk."

"I will walk out of here. Lord only knows how they got me into this predicament to start."

Abby shot a look at Riley. "They?"

"Yes. I made the coffee and started up to bed and there they were, right in my living room."

"You saw their faces?"

"No," she said, shaking her head. The gesture threw her off balance, but Riley steadied her. "They had black ski masks on."

"We saw the mess in your house," Abby said. "You put up quite a fight."

"I clocked one of them in the knee with that hickory stick I keep in the umbrella stand."

Riley made a mental note to watch for someone with a fresh limp. He could tell by the way Abby's eyebrows arched that she was thinking the same thing and would pass that detail on to every shift and the extra patrols.

The radios he and Abby were wearing crackled as verification came from other teams that the other bombs were neutralized without any casualties. No sign of additional hostages. That was something anyway. Even without a bomb squad on-site they'd managed to clear the area and ensure that the explosions intended to kill and maim had harmed no one.

As the paramedics met them, Riley caught Abby's hand. "Thanks for the cover fire."

"Least I could do," she said.

"What do you carry?" She showed him the .40 caliber gun. "Nice," he said with a smile.

Abby shrugged, her attention darting all around.

"What's wrong?"

"He blew himself up, I think," she said quietly. She clamped her lips together, breathing deep through her nose. "I fired at his feet. A warning shot. But he..."

Riley didn't want her thinking about that gruesome blood smear on the rocks. "Did you recognize him? Was he limping?"

"No." She shook her head. "His face was painted with camouflage and he wore green patterned gear. I didn't recognize anything about him. As for the limp, who could tell on this terrain?"

True. "The feds will be all over this."

"I know." Her shoulders hitched and she rubbed at her arms. "I never thought I'd be grateful for their help. This is one crime scene I'm happy to turn over."

"It's over." Hopefully for good, but at least for the moment.

She nodded. "We'll have to give statements. I have all kinds of paperwork." She swore. "And a press conference."

"Then we'd best get at it." He gestured for her to lead the way to the docks.

"I'm a mess," she complained, picking a twig from her sleeve. "This sweater isn't worth giving away."

He reached out and pulled a leaf from her hair. "You're beautiful." He wanted to kiss her, to reassure himself she was safe and in one piece.

"You're just saying that to make me feel better."

"I'm saying it because it's the truth." He waited, cradling her hands in his until she finally looked at him. Her eyes went wide, then she smiled and looked away. "Your department, hell, the whole town, should throw you a parade. You're a hero, Abby."

"You did the hard part," she argued.

"Don't dodge the compliment."

"Fine." She took a big breath and looked out over the water one last time. "But I'm a hero with a ton of paperwork to do."

He was damn happy that they were all alive to do that paperwork. Today had been too close.

ABBY TURNED FROM the podium and the crush of questions, letting Mayor Scott finish things up. During this press conference, she'd been more careful with her words without compromising her determination. She would not allow this nonsense to continue in her town. Having Mrs. Wilks home safe had done just the opposite of what her enemies wanted. The rescue boosted her popularity. Even if he'd wanted to, the mayor wouldn't be able to oust her now.

It should give her comfort, but instead she worried over how things could get worse. Who might end up a victim next? She couldn't afford to think about that here, where the cameras might capture the worry on her face. Most of the reporters were still asking questions about the man who'd driven Mrs. Wilks's car into the bay.

They weren't alone. She had more than a few questions for Riley O'Brien, too. Though she would be forever grateful for what he'd done, how had a construction worker turned Christmas-decorating guru known how to disarm a bomb?

The mayor deflected the hard questions and tailored his answers to suit his purposes. He'd dubbed Riley the hero of Belclare, telling everyone Riley had gone to the hospital simply as a precaution, and the mayor would be stopping there next. Yes, of course the mayor and town council would be looking into honoring Belclare's newest hero in the coming days.

It went on and on. Abby listened enough to applaud or nod stoically in the right places. The most she would get out of this was a lesson in managing the press. At last they were done and she retreated into the station while the mayor's team cleaned up the podium.

"Nicely done, Jensen." Mayor Scott shook her hand, adding a pat on her shoulder.

Despite having taken a shower and changed into a clean suit, she felt weary and frustrated. The last thing she needed was a political shadow. "It was a group effort," she replied. Right now, she wanted that group scouring security footage. Two men had attacked Mrs. Wilks, but only one was dead. She needed to find the other man to help her break up what she now felt confident was a local terrorist cell.

When the mayor was done shaking hands, she and her officers were able to get busy. Abby settled behind a spare desk, her gaze drifting over the plastic sheeting that blocked off the burned side of the building. The cleaning crew claimed they would finish today, but fresh paint and new equipment was only the first part. The emotional impact would stay with her and the department for weeks, if not longer. In her gut, she knew that was the real motivation behind the fire.

She slipped the flash drive into her computer and

started another search through Filmore's life. Who—local or otherwise—could have compelled him to set that fire?

Her gaze skimmed from her laptop screen and out across the bullpen. It took a concerted effort to resist the tug of paranoia and go back to the facts in front of her.

"Chief!" She looked up again as Gadsden waved her over. "I've got the wallet getting tossed at the warehouse Dumpster."

With a fresh surge of energy, she hurried over to Gadsden. "Praise God for detail-oriented people."

Gadsden pointed out the wallet sailing through the air.

"Great. Now we back it up. There has to be something that shows us a bit more," she said, praying it was true.

"This gives us a timeline," he replied, pointing at the date and time in the corner of the video. "The car and Mrs. Wilks had to have been staged before this point."

Abby nodded. As leads went, she'd seen stronger, but it was a starting point. "And that looks like a blatant attempt to implicate Ri—Mr. O'Brien or one of his coworkers."

"Yeah," Gadsden agreed. "Good bet the scarf was planted rather than an accident. Who would've guessed you'd be his alibi."

She pointedly ignored that comment. "See if there are other views or angles around the docks in this time frame." She wanted the second assailant. Her hands fisted at her sides. "I want faces. No one should feel that comfortable causing havoc in this town."

"You know, it's possible Mr. O'Brien knew what to do with those bombs because he *is* involved."

"Show me more evidence and we'll follow it," she said. Just because Gadsden was right didn't mean she had to like it. During the crisis, she'd led by example as they'd followed and eliminated the evidence already planted against Riley.

She would continue to do her job, no matter how sticky or uncomfortable things got.

Gadsden was right, however. Riley had shown awareness and expertise that only came from training and experience. He owed her answers. Now she just had to smother her feelings and find the objectivity and courage to ask the right questions.

The calm professionalism that had earned her this post was crumbling to pieces inside her, though she refused to let it show. She wanted to slam doors. Throw things. Shoot something. Declare a police emergency and conduct a door-to-door search. She nearly laughed, thinking about how the mayor would spin that.

Their best lead had blown himself up, a fanatic so dedicated he preferred suicide over capture. It wasn't a good sign of things to come. And yet, to the best of her knowledge no one in Belclare was missing.

The other caches of explosives along the shoreline had blown within a minute of the sniper. That detail alone strongly indicated a supervisor with an impatient trigger finger. Her instincts wouldn't let her chalk it up to blind luck. It was a miracle no one on the search teams had been seriously injured. Only Riley's quick work and the note he'd salvaged had saved no telling how many lives.

Was his finding that note part of the plan, too?

She shook off the thought and looked around the station. The men and women who served the Belclare police department were top-notch, but there simply weren't enough of them to patrol every high-risk area every hour of the day. The docks were a valuable target. Main Street, packed with tourists, would certainly make the news if something bad happened. She forced herself to imagine the worst-case scenario if this cell launched an attack when the park was full of families.

She'd appealed to the community to keep watch and report anything suspicious, praising the dock workers and giving them much of the credit for today's rescue operation. Without that kind of vigilance and action, she'd said, Mrs. Wilks might have died.

"We'll track 'em down, Chief."

Gadsden's assurance snapped her from her thoughts, but it would be a long time before she relaxed. "Yes," she agreed. "We will track down every last one of them."

Returning to her temporary desk, she noticed a new email in-box alert flashing on her screen. Sinking into the chair, anticipating the worst, she clicked on it.

Congratulations, Chief Jensen. You win today's skirmish but this war isn't over.

There was an attachment. Against her better judgment, she opened it. A three-panel cartoon strip filled the screen. First a caricature of the bandstand in the park, then that picture overlaid with animated flames. The last panel was a sad little pile of ash topped with an oversize police shield sporting her badge number.

They'd do it. She felt it in her gut. This opening weekend or not, they had the will and resources to make her worst nightmare come true.

"Cowards," she whispered to herself. "Bring it on." She sent the file up the line to the federal agencies that were supposedly doing something helpful behind the scenes to break up the sleeper cell they had suspected from the beginning was in Belclare. While she was grateful the federal teams were taking care of all the bomb evidence out by the water, anytime they wanted to step in with some real, boots-on-the-ground help, that would be fine by her.

She leaned back, the springs on the worn-out chair

squeaking in protest. Her department was crammed into half of their normal working space. Filmore had protected the building's facade but wreaked havoc inside. Her officers were tired and more than a little edgy with all of the reacting they'd been doing.

They were stretched too thin with the extra patrols, and asking them to maintain that level indefinitely was unacceptable. She needed a new play, something offensive that would bring this war to a head. For her department, as well as for the community at large.

If the terrorist cell could create chaos using people from petty criminals to snipers to historical society presidents, she could sure as hell plan a resounding victory with the people on her side. Assuming there were people on her side.

That list seemed terribly short. Maybe it was better to use a neutral party.

For the potentially crazy idea that popped into her mind, a neutral party, one well versed in personal defense, was her best option. Her only option. She ran her fingertips along on the edge of the desk. She shouldn't do it, shouldn't put any civilians in the line of fire for any reason. Except the terrorists had done that for her and they didn't show the first inclination of stopping.

The Lewiston family lived outside Belclare town limits and took advantage of the fact at every opportunity. Since becoming the Belclare police chief she'd tossed out more than one citation for an illegal whiskey still. The Lewistons just didn't buy into the concept of law enforcement on private property. They were all excellent game hunters, blessed with perfect aim, and her officers knew firsthand they were always armed.

But each December the family got their legal act together and assembled the proper permits because the ideal place for their Christmas tree sales lot straddled a narrow smidge of the town line. Their reputation for offering the finest trees in three counties drew record numbers of buyers every year. Alongside the Christmas Village, it had become a symbiotic partnership benefiting both the Lewiston family and Belclare.

She flipped back through her file of threatening emails, finding the one she'd mentioned to Riley about the Christmas tree lot. No, it hadn't been anything overt or direct, but the threat was phrased by someone who knew the Lewiston reputation for trouble the other eleven months of the year.

Damn it.

She should have considered that before, but now she would use it to her advantage. Resting her hands lightly on her keyboard, she measured her words carefully. If she could draw out the person planning all of this chaos, she could bring this to an end before anyone else—tourist or resident—got hurt.

There was no way to know for sure that the email would be read by the right person in time, but she had to try. When she was absolutely certain her invitation presented the perfect combination of bravado and temptation, she hit Send. As the message crossed cyberspace to the three most frequent addresses used on her hate mail, she murmured a prayer.

It was possible the feds would also catch wind of her idea, but it was a risk she had to take. To do nothing, to let this terrorist cell keep chipping away at her friends, her town and her confidence was intolerable. At least the Lewiston family could aptly defend themselves.

"Let's have our own merry Christmas," she muttered. "I'll bring a one-size-fits-all ticket to prison for you." She gathered her computer, cell phone and purse and said goodbye to everyone for the evening, but she didn't go straight home.

Taking her time, she drove out to see the welcome sign, admiring the creative display that set the mood for the tourists she hoped would arrive en masse tomorrow.

Coming back through the center of town, she felt like a little kid as she passed each display. Transformed, each street had an individual holiday theme, ranging from fanciful to elegant. The decorating teams had delivered yet again. Because they were outsiders it would be so easy to blame the vendors and temporary workers for the trouble, but she knew better. Her instincts told her the root of this crime wave was local.

Filmore would be impressed and pleased with the end results and, for a moment, she entertained the idea of snapping a picture of Main Street to take to him. She drove out to the park instead. The ironwork at the park entrance had been lit with white lights and the garland wound with sparkling ribbon, much like the lampposts on her neighborhood street.

Thoughts of Riley followed her as she slowly moved through the park. He'd shown both heroism and expertise today at the dock. He'd revealed an interest and awareness of her work most men didn't possess.

Maybe, as he'd said, he was just in the right place at the right time. Maybe he did plan to stay in Belclare because he liked the town. And when pigs started flying maybe she would believe him just because he kissed her so well.

There was more to the man and his story. As her pulse sped up, she realized exactly how eager she was to have some answers. Not only for the Wilks case, but for herself.

Snow started falling as Abby reached the bandstand and this time she did pull over and park. Vendor booths were scattered around behind the sloped green where Belclare residents enjoyed concerts and performances by the community theater. Santa Claus and his elves would take requests from ten to four. The Ferris wheel would run all day and into the night for the next three weeks, its colorful lights a beacon of holiday happiness.

She would not let anyone wreck that for the citizens she protected or for the tourists.

Getting out of her car, she enjoyed the utter quiet as big fat flakes caught in her hair and eyelashes. After soaking up the peaceful moment and letting it restore her battered nerves, she used her phone to take a few pictures. But she already knew the truth. The sick little cartoon from her email had been drawn up based on this year's bandstand display.

Provided the tourists were brave enough to come out despite the troubles in Belclare, tomorrow this area of the park would be crowded with people enjoying the carnival atmosphere in this winter wonderland. And if everything went according to plan at the Christmas tree lot, they would safely enjoy the experience and have happy memories to cherish.

Satisfied she could pull off her plans, she drove home. Turning into her neighborhood, she passed house after house with decorated Christmas trees in the windows. She really needed to put up her tree.

It seemed every front window on her street sported a decorated tree. Calder's window had a tree blooming with colorful lights and, without taking a closer look, Abby knew it would be sporting lengths of paper chains and macaroni garlands made by the excited hands of a happy child.

She pulled into her driveway and stopped her car next to Riley's truck. He'd plugged in the lights for her outdoor display, but her empty window looked like the Grinch had come by. Even Mrs. Wilks and Riley had managed to decorate their trees today despite bombs, hospital visits and police reports.

There was nothing more she could do tonight to net the terrorist cell. She might as well get busy and pull down the artificial tree from the attic.

The light came on over Riley's back door and she watched, mesmerized with the way his body moved as he stomped into his boots and slipped his arms through the red vest he always wore.

He walked up to her car and reached for the door handle. She hit the unlock button and let him open the door for her. "Such service," she said, stepping into the cold air.

"I've been watching for you," he said, a wide smile on his face. "You looked great at the press conference."

The snow fell on his hair and shoulders, sparkling before melting.

"Thanks. Weren't you at the hospital?"

"Sure, but they released me right away." He held out his hands for her inspection, but she was looking at the scrapes on his face. "Just a few scratches."

The criminals had called this a skirmish, but Riley's face had taken a beating. She reached out, not quite touching the butterfly closures across one lean cheekbone. It was a miracle his eyes had been spared.

Riley turned his face and brushed his lips across her palm. "I have a surprise for you." He walked backward toward his house, as if he couldn't stand to take his eyes off her.

Feeling inordinately flattered by that, she felt herself smiling back at him. Until an echo of Gadsden's voice intruded with the reminder that Riley might be working for the terrorists, too. "Why?"

"I need a reason?"

Everyone had reasons and agendas for the things they did. She didn't want to cloud the moment with work and worry, but she didn't want to be a fool if his handsome face hid a sinister purpose. "I guess not."

"Wow. You must be tired."

"Why do you say that?" She stepped forward, hopelessly drawn to him despite the risk. Maybe because of it. She told herself she was just anticipating the surprise.

"You gave up the questioning too quickly." His eyebrows bobbed up and down. "I was kind of expecting an interrogation."

"All right." He'd opened the door and she had to follow through. "What are you up to?" *Way to start strong, Abby.*

He grinned. "Wait right there. Don't move."

"Uh-huh." She folded her arms across her chest, hoping she wasn't being a complete idiot.

He disappeared behind the house and worry clogged her throat when she heard a scrape and rustle. "Are you okay?" Should she go for her gun or just dive in to provide backup for whatever he'd encountered?

"I'm fine," he called. "Stay put."

Fine. "I saw Mrs. Wilks got her tree up and…" She lost her train of thought as Riley came back into view. Or rather, as an enormous, fresh fir tree came into view, propelled by Riley's untied boots. "What's that?"

He leaned around the tree. "It's a *real* Christmas tree." His smile chased away every question and doubt hanging over her. No one harboring ill intent could look so happy over something as sentimental as a Christmas tree. Completely weak as rationalizations went, she let instinct have its way. That single expression changed her whole evening, erasing the turmoil of the criminal element plaguing her town.

The rich scent of the fresh-cut evergreen rolled over her, renewing her in the quiet snowfall. "It's huge."

"Mrs. Wilks helped me pick out all three of them at the Lewiston farm. She said they always have the best trees."

She swallowed down a resurgence of fresh doubt at the coincidence. "Three?"

"Yeah. One for her, one for me, and this one for you."

"I saw the windows when I pulled in," she said.

"We've probably been almost as busy as you." He set the tree down between them. "Of course, we've definitely had more fun. If you don't want it I'll find it another home."

"I want it," she said quickly. "It's perfect." She returned to her car for her purse to hide the unexpected nerves flooding her system. It had been such a long day and this was the perfect way to wrap it up. Or maybe she was losing her mind and had surrendered to the inevitable.

He looked the tree up and down. "I picked up a new tree stand since I couldn't be sure where yours was."

"Sounds like you thought of everything."

He hitched a shoulder. "I'm a detail guy."

"Yes. I've noticed." She unlocked her back door and let him wrestle the tree inside.

"Which way?"

"Down the hall and to the left."

She was impressed when he didn't knock anything over or off the walls as he maneuvered down the narrow hallway. It brought back an unwelcome reminder of the mess they'd found at Mrs. Wilks's house.

Another realization struck her, but she waited until he had the tree safely leaning between a chair and the wall. "You took her tree-shopping and helped her decorate to keep an eye on her, didn't you?"

He slipped his hands into his pockets. "Guilty as charged."

"I bet you even helped her clean up the mess in her house."

He shrugged. "Is that a problem?"

"No." It was thoughtful. Kind.

"She's one tough lady," he said. "But no one should deal with that alone. Besides, she gave me more cookies."

"Lucky man," Abby said, laughing. She was enjoying the normalcy of this moment. Standing here with him, she had the strangest sensation things might be okay. Who'd have guessed a stranger could make her feel this safe and stable in the midst of such a violent assault on Belclare?

"I'll just go get the tree stand."

"How does leftover lasagna sound?"

His gaze locked with hers, then drifted slowly to her mouth. She hoped it meant he wanted to kiss her as much as she wanted to kiss him.

"Delicious."

"Okay. I'll—" she hitched her thumb over her shoulder to the kitchen "—just get started on that while you put the tree in water."

Riley didn't move right away. He looked around the room. "You want it centered in the window, right?"

"Please."

"I can do that." He looked at her ceiling, then her furniture. Then his eyes landed on the flowers from Deke on her coffee table. His eyebrows snapped together in a hard scowl. "An admirer?" He tipped his head to the lavish arrangement.

"Not even close," she said. Her warm mood burst like a bubble. "It was a friendly gesture from Deke Maynard."

"Sure."

She slipped out of her coat and hooked it on the hall tree at the front door. Deke was the furthest thing from her mind with Riley filling up her front room. "It was meant as encouragement."

"That's some serious encouragement," he said softly. "You know, if I'm poaching here—"

"Poaching?" She cut him off, bristling at the archaic choice of words. "I'm not endangered wildlife, Riley."

"You know that's not what I meant."

She planted her hands on her hips. "One minute you're buying me a Christmas tree—with a stand—and the next you think I'm playing around or something."

He stepped forward but stopped when she held out a hand. "That is not what I meant."

"Then clear it up right now," she demanded.

"I like you." He took another step, stopping just as his chest brushed her fingers. "I want you," he added, his gaze hot on her. "I go after what I want, what I like. Sometimes I come on a little strong."

Her mind reeled at his speech. Her indignation faded. She was more surprised her knees didn't buckle. He was an arm's length away and her imagination leaped into overdrive, her mind on how his hands and mouth would feel if he closed the distance and kissed her. Did men come any hotter than this one? "I kissed you first," she muttered. "That should have been a clue."

His mouth twitched. "I remember. But I'm new in town and I don't know all the dynamics. What I do know is that I don't like sharing."

Where this was coming from dawned on her then. "Danny told you I meet with Deke every week."

Riley bobbed his head, but his eyes didn't leave hers.

"It's coffee. As friends." She reached back and pulled out the pins holding her hair up in a bun. Slipping the pins into her pocket, she raked her hands through her hair. It didn't escape her notice how Riley's eyes tracked every move. "He's talented, and very shy. He's also extremely influential."

"I heard the ads."

"Precisely my point. He's been very supportive. The flowers were a nice surprise from a friend."

"He delivered them personally?"

It seemed an odd thing for him to latch on to. "You just delivered a tree," she pointed out. "Deke is only a friend." She might have briefly hoped for more, but in the presence of Riley she understood exactly how lonely she'd been. Deke might have eventually been more, but not now. "It was important to me to maintain that friendship for Belclare."

"Got it."

"Do you?"

"Yes." He raised her hand from his chest to his lips. "You are a brave, gorgeous woman. Can you blame me for assuming there was competition?"

She rolled her eyes, though the compliment warmed her from head to toe. She pulled her hands free. Giving in to temptation, she leaned forward and kissed his cheek. "Go get the stand. I'll get dinner."

"Yes, ma'am."

"You don't ever have to say that to me again," she said, leading him back down the hall to the kitchen.

She found an apron to protect her skirt and kept herself on task, starting the oven and prepping a salad to go with the leftover lasagna. It was a comfortable time as Riley worked, bringing in the tree stand and a handsaw. A prepared man was a treasure, she thought absently as she slid the lasagna into the oven.

Riley called her to the front room for an opinion. "Well?"

"It's beautiful." She wasn't sure how, but he'd managed to find the perfect tree. It fit the space beautifully. "You sure don't waste any time."

"The present is all we're guaranteed."

The pragmatic philosophy reminded her that she'd likely

stirred up a brand-new hornets' nest before she'd left the station. Tomorrow could very well be her professional downfall if she'd overplayed her hand in that email.

"How much time before dinner's ready?"

She checked her watch. "Fifteen more minutes."

"Great. Point me to your decorations and I'll pull down the boxes."

"I can do that tomorrow," she protested. "You've really done enough."

"I'm on a roll here," he said with that dead-sexy grin. "If Mrs. Wilks and I can decorate two trees—"

"She helped you decorate your tree?" He really had been keeping an eye on the older woman. His kindness created a warmth inside Abby that had been missing in recent weeks.

"The cookies went to my head," he replied.

"Right." Abby started up the stairs. "I keep the boxes of decorations in the attic."

She tried not to think about how close he was as his boots sounded on the steps behind her. The man sent her system into overdrive with just a look. *The present is all we're guaranteed.* His words echoed in her head, mocking her, tempting her. If leaving the lasagna wasn't risking a fire, she might have taken him on an immediate and *present* detour to her bedroom.

She pulled down the access door in the ceiling and unfolded the steps. "Christmas boxes are just to the right."

Squeezing around him, she headed back downstairs. "Riley?" He paused on the steps. "Thanks."

"Your lasagna is well worth it."

There he went, lightening the mood and putting her at ease.

She returned to the kitchen with a smile on her face and had a quick debate over which table to set. The kitchen felt too casual and the dining room felt like too much pressure.

She split the difference with green place mats and a votive centered on a bright red napkin on the kitchen table. It felt like something out of a magazine from the 1950s, but she heard Riley in the hallway and knew she didn't have time to start over.

"THAT'S QUITE A VIGNETTE," Riley said, pausing in the doorway and taking it all in. It was a significant part of his job in Belclare to keep an eye on her, but it was a major perk, too. He'd told her the truth: he liked her. In uniform. In a firefight on the shore. Looking elegant in the ivory shirt, black skirt and heels that she wore right now.

He liked kissing her. And talking with her. Even arguing over bombs or flowers. "Smells even better the second time around," he said, searching for a way to get his mind back on the matter at hand. He needed to know if she'd learned anything about the dead sniper or the men who'd kidnapped Mrs. Wilks.

With the Christmas Village officially opening tomorrow, it would be easier if they could narrow the search parameters beyond ruling out Calder and Mrs. Wilks. He probably shouldn't have spent so many hours babysitting Mrs. Wilks, but he'd learned a lot just from listening to the woman chatter.

"Thanks. Have a seat," Abby said. "Do you want wine?"

"No, thanks." He watched her pour a generous glass for herself. He peered around her to the oven timer. Six minutes was enough time. "Do you mind if I grab a beer from my place?"

"Not at all."

He went next door as fast as he could without running until he got inside. Then he pounded up the stairs and changed into khakis and a button-down. He'd cleaned up after the ordeal on the shore, of course, but he'd been dealing with fresh pine trees and dusty boxes the rest of the day. Dressed the way she was, she deserved to share the meal with a man wearing something better than his work jeans and thermal shirt. It was the excuse he was sticking with anyway. He was too rushed to review his sudden urge to impress her. He brushed the dust out of his hair and then found his socks and deck shoes.

When he returned to her kitchen door, beer in hand, she was pulling the casserole dish out of the oven. She set it on the table and looked up, her jaw dropping. "What... You didn't have to...get all dressed up."

"Yeah, I did," he replied. The way she looked at him proved it a hundred times over. He came around and pulled out her chair, noticing the level in the wineglass was the same, but the lipstick print at the rim was new.

So he wasn't the only one dealing with a few nerves. Nice. The big question remained—were her nerves a residual from the tumultuous day or somehow related to him? He decided he could deal with the combination as long as he was a contributing factor.

She started the small talk as they filled their plates and he kept the conversation light, as well. While he wanted to know about the issues with the case, he respected that she needed a little distance.

"You look great," she said as she assembled a small bite of salad on her fork.

"Thanks." He'd noticed she wasn't eating, just sort of moving her food around on her plate, but he didn't think his wardrobe change was the cause. "What's distracting you?"

"Nothing. Everything." She poked at another piece of romaine lettuce and rolled a cherry tomato on top, but she didn't put it in her mouth.

"I'm a good listener."

"I've noticed." She looked up, smiling. "But this isn't the time."

He took a sip of beer. "Offer stands. You know where to find me."

"True."

He cast around for a better distraction. "Are you picky about stringing lights?"

Her gaze narrowed at him. "Define picky."

"Well." He pushed his plate back and leaned forward a bit. "In my experience there are three kinds of people when it comes to Christmas lights."

"Do tell."

"There are those who don't care how the job gets done. Then there are those who are picky about something. Either the amount of wiring that shows or starting at the top versus the bottom. You get the idea."

She nodded, her mouth full of salad.

Progress. "Then there are the insane types who are morally opposed to anything less than their personal definition of lighting perfection. A precise balance across every branch, the cords all arranged out of sight and connected at the back of the tree... Well, you get the idea."

"Yes." She paused, filling her mouth with a big bite of lasagna.

"Mrs. Wilks is picky in a sweet, traditional way. She likes white lights that go from the bottom to the top, casting her angel tree topper in a halo of light."

"Well said." She raised her glass to him. "You like colored lights."

"To be fair, those were left over from one of the displays. No time to shop, so I bought them from my boss yesterday."

"What will you do for ornaments?"

"Peg had a decent selection at the hardware store. Thought I'd go by tomorrow." That put the tension right back in her face. Damn. He mentally scrambled. "When I was a kid, each grade level took turns decorating the big Christmas tree in the narthex each year."

"Based on what you've done to Belclare you must have loved it."

"Not when Sister Mary Catherine was in charge. She was one of the insane types when it came to stringing lights. For the sake of the children I hope someone eventually donates a pre-lit fake tree to the church."

She relaxed enough to chuckle at the story and he was relieved to share something real about his past with her. "Are you going to answer the question?"

She pushed her chair back from the table and carried her wineglass to the counter. Mischief flashed in her eyes as she watched him. "What will you do if I admit I'm an insane sort?"

"I'll let you string them yourself."

"No problem. I've done it before. Every year of my adult life, in fact."

"Sounds like you have a system. Maybe I'll learn something new," he said, matching her teasing tone as he picked up their plates.

She moved forward to take them. "You don't have to clean up."

"I know." In her heels, she was almost eye level with him. He leaned in and kissed her. The contact was just a soft meeting of lips, nothing involved or intense, but it rocked his world all the same. "You cooked. I'll clean."

She shot him a look full of suspicion. "Either your mother raised you well or two trees are too much for you in one day."

"Could be both," he replied, grinning. "And you did mention all that experience."

"I did." She stepped back, raised her hands in surrender. "You clean, I'll string. Just out of pity for you."

He cleaned up the table and dishes in record time. Not only did he want to watch her process, but he remembered too late that the tree would ruin her shirt. When he reached the front room, he found her on her knees by the outlet under the window, the lit string of colored lights in her hands apparently forgotten. She was staring past the tree toward Calder's house, surely reliving her friend's accident.

The snow was coming down a little heavier now and would really set the mood for the Christmas Village in the morning. Belclare couldn't have wished for better weather and he was surprised by how much he hoped the sudden crime spree didn't hurt the event.

This place, after such a short time, felt more like home than anywhere he'd been before. He looked to Abby and knew she was a big part of the reason.

"Hey," he said gently, not wanting to startle her.

She turned and the hard expression in her eyes startled him. This wasn't a woman mourning a friend's pain or struggling with guilt that she might be part of the cause. No, that was sheer determination in her eyes.

"You've done something," he said without thinking.

"What?" She blinked rapidly and her expression cleared. "No. I just don't know where to start."

"Bull." He dropped to his knee beside her. "You barely remember why you're in here."

"That's rude."

"Rude might just be the beginning," he corrected. "Hand over the lights before you ruin your shirt."

"I can do it."

"I know, Abby." She could do whatever she set her mind to. Which worried him considering what she was up against. He wanted her to tell him, but why would she?

As far as she knew he was only a carpenter with some life experience. "But I bet you don't normally string lights dressed like that. Test the next string."

"Riley."

"What? There's no shame in accepting a little help." He couldn't look at her. He was too close to offering her more truth than she needed. More than he was allowed to share.

Eyeing the distance from the tree to the outlet, he started weaving lights through the lower branches at record speed. His hands knew what to do, which was nice considering he had no idea how to proceed with Abby.

"Riley?"

He adjusted the cord so the connector would be hidden. "Next string." He held out his free hand, but nothing landed in it.

"Look at me."

He sat back on his heels. "My pleasure." He tried to focus on her, just her, not his irrational fear for her safety. She'd kicked off her shoes and her feet were tucked under her, the skirt riding just above her knees.

"I was thinking about what you said, that we only have the present."

"Okay." He didn't know what to do with his empty hands. Was that a veiled invitation to demand professional answers or personal pleasure? There was nothing in her gaze or body language to clue him in. "I can work on the tree lights in the present."

"You can." Her smile was slow and lovely in the soft light of the lamp in the corner. She put the next strand of lights in his hand.

Grateful for the distraction, he went back to the task.

"You're a man of many talents," she said carefully. "Can you tell me where you learned about bombs?"

Officially, the answer was no. "I learned about explosives on the job," he said, choosing not to specify which job.

"But we didn't open that trunk and find explosives. You found wires. And the note."

"Wires that didn't belong. Wires that led to explosives. The note was meant to be found. If not by me, then by you or another officer." He risked a look over his shoulder, catching the thoughtful crease between her brows. Someone had made her doubt him when she didn't really want to. He resumed stringing each branch with lights. "Explosives are used in a number of construction situations. I've had my share of experience handling those situations. Truth is, I know a little something about a lot of things, Abby. Cars, flooring, garland. It's why I took the job here." Another nugget of truth, though he doubted she'd ever willingly forgive him for the omission. "It's why I took on the Hamilton house."

"Okay."

He finished with that strand and plugged it into the previous one. "Plug it in," he said, nodding to the outlet. "Let's see if you're happy so far."

On hands and knees, she gave his resolve one hell of a test as she plugged it in. He turned his gaze to the tree before she caught him lusting after the sweet, ripe curve of her backside.

"Wow," she whispered. "It's lovely."

Man of many talents, he thought. "I'm thinking you're less picky and more the easygoing type."

"You wish," she said. "Forgive the interrogation. You were just cucumber-cool with everything today, I thought maybe you'd spent time as a cop or…"

"A criminal?"

"They are known to wander."

"Would a criminal have helped Mrs. Wilks?"

"No, but a con man might."

He'd walked right into that one. "Well, she does make a chocolate-chip cookie worth reforming for, but I'm neither criminal nor con man."

"No. According to Mayor Scott, you're the hero of Belclare."

He choked on that moniker. "I could go the rest of my life without having those words aimed at me," he said. "You can trust me, Abby." If anyone in Belclare was on her side, it was him. "Let's finish this." He was referring to more than the tree.

"Maybe I don't trust myself," she admitted, handing him more lights. "Every time I turn around something else is damaged or someone else is in jeopardy."

"You got the win today."

She snorted and started pacing across the room behind him. "No one to question is hardly a victory. They didn't recover any helpful prints at Mrs. Wilks's house."

"Has Filmore offered anything more?"

"No."

Her impatience was disconcerting. He'd bet his fake cover story family and their shepherd's pie that she'd done something drastic. "I trust you," he said. "So do Mrs. Wilks, Calder, Peg, your department. They aren't idiots, Abby, and you don't have to be a lifelong resident of Belclare to see they rely on you because they know they can."

He wrestled his way through the middle section of the tree, grateful that it kept him from reaching for her. She had to bring him a stepladder to finish the top, but he could tell she was pleased when the job was done.

"I hate stringing lights," she said.

"Happy to help."

"Whether I start at the top or the bottom," she continued, "I always get irritated and careless before the job is done."

"That sounds really out of character for you."

"It's one place patience fails me." Laughing at herself, she handed him a star for the top of the tree.

"Don't you want to put it on?"

She shook her head. "You're already there."

"All right." He secured the star to the top and stepped down, setting the ladder to the side so it would be there when she put on the ornaments. "Looks good, if I do say so myself."

She pulled the drapes across the window. "I agree." But she was staring at him, not the tree. "You have sap on your shirt." She came closer and pointed to the offending spot.

"It'll wash."

"It's not your only good shirt?"

"No." Though most of his clothes were in storage while he sorted out where he'd live in Belclare.

"That's good." She reached out and yanked his shirt open, sending buttons flying.

"Abby?"

"I'm living in the present," she said. "I've always wanted to do that, but until you, I haven't been inspired." Her hands, warm and soft, flattened against his bare chest. "Tell me you're surprised. Please?" She pressed up on her toes, her lips brushing fleetingly against his.

"Surprised?" Then he remembered her words last night in the truck. "Oh, yeah." He wrapped her in his arms and pulled her close, the silk of her shirt an enticing, filmy barrier against his skin. Slowly, taking his time instead of just taking, he lowered his mouth to meet hers.

Her lips were soft and needy, and when her tongue stroked against his it was sweeter than it had been last night. She tasted of the deep red wine she'd had at dinner, a dark, sultry counterbalance to the crisp pine and sweet roses scenting the air.

She pushed the shirt over his shoulders and down his arms. Reluctantly, he released her to shake free of the binding fabric. He was nearly ready to beg, desperately eager to learn everything about her body, about how well it would fit with his. He wanted to discover what she liked and more, what made her absolutely crazy with passion.

Her hands molded and caressed his arms while he feathered kisses along the side of her neck, nipping gently at the warm curve of her shoulder.

She tempted him to rush with her kisses, her touch and her soft sighs. "Abby," he whispered against her skin. His blood pounded through his veins. If there had ever been another woman, he couldn't remember it.

There was only her, here and now in this moment. He skimmed his hand up her ribs to cup her full breast. With a moan, she arched into his touch and he felt her nipple pebble against his palm. He couldn't wait to taste her.

He heard the soft purr of a zipper followed by the rustle of fabric as her skirt fell to the floor. Ready to protest as she stepped away from him, the view stole his breath and he couldn't form the words. Lace-topped stockings caressed each thigh and the creamy skin above invited a thorough exploration.

She came back to him and wound her arms around his neck. He hitched her up until those long thighs circled his hips. He turned, bracing her back against the wall. Happily, he'd take her right here, or on the couch—hell, even the steps looked good.

All of the above. All in good time.

He carried her to the couch and sank into the cushions, her legs straddling his thighs, all of her open to his touch. He peeled away her shirt and trailed his fingers along the straps of her bra. When he unhooked it and let the lingerie fall away, he held her, learning how she wanted to be touched.

He set out to show her how beautiful she was to him. How she made him feel so wanted. Skimming his hands over every inch of her flesh, he showed her what she meant. He pulled her close, taking first one breast then the other into his mouth, teasing her soft flesh with tongue and teeth. Her palms were braced on his shoulders, and her little moans were sweet encouragement.

She shifted away, bringing her mouth down to his. The kiss turned into a sensual dual as her tongue slid across his. Her hands cruised over his chest and lower until he was rocking his erection into her delicious touch.

As she opened his slacks, taking him in hand, he slipped a finger under that lace and found her wet, hot and ready. Need surged through him. "Abby." He raised up, stripping away his clothing. The only remaining barrier was her panties. With a wink, he reached out and tore them away.

Wearing only her thigh-highs, she came over him, gliding down slowly until she'd taken him fully inside her. He waited, holding back by some miracle, while she set the pace. It was worth the wait—when she moved it was heaven. Gripping her hips, he met her body with each stroke, until her climax shuddered through her and around him, her fingertips digging into his shoulders.

His release came a moment later and she dropped her head against his shoulder, panting and snuggling close as they floated back to reality.

After a few minutes she shifted again. "Told you the couch is too small." She stood up, keeping his hands in hers. "Come share my bed."

He didn't know it was possible to go from completely sated to all-out need in the span of one staircase, but it happened.

When they reached her bedroom her tender kiss ignited an encore performance that stole his breath. Spent, her body felt as pliable as butter sprawled across his chest. He heard her whispering softly against his skin but couldn't make out the words. "What was that?" he asked.

She raised her head, propping her chin on her hands to meet his gaze. "'Soul meets soul on lovers' lips.'"

He ran a finger down her spine. "You're quoting Shelley?"

"It seems to fit." Her smile was nothing short of radiant. "You know the quote."

"I do."

"You consistently surprise me, Riley."

He combed his hand through her hair. "Same goes, Abby."

She pulled the covers over them and snuggled next to him. "I'm glad you're here."

"Me, too." He pressed a kiss to her hair and listened to the simple perfection of her breath until she fell asleep.

Chapter Fourteen

Abby slipped from the bed, careful not to disturb Riley. He was sprawled facedown across the mattress, the tangled sheets leaving him more exposed than covered. Of all her recent challenges, exiting the bed proved the most difficult.

With a wistful sigh, she kept moving. She'd make it up to him later. Tonight, after they had the terrorist in custody, they could celebrate. They could even go down to the park and join the fun of a successful opening day of the Christmas Village.

She found dark jeans and a sweater and dressed in the guest room so she wouldn't wake him. Then she wrote him a note and left it on her pillow. If she was lucky, this would all be over before he realized she was gone.

Optimism was a good thing.

WHEN RILEY HEARD Abby leave the house he opened his eyes. Rolling over, he stared at her bedroom ceiling, only moving after he heard the low rumble of her car engine. Still he waited until the noise faded before he rolled out of the bed.

He supposed he should be flattered she trusted him enough to leave him alone in her house. This was, after all, the opportunity he'd wanted since arriving in Belclare. He reclaimed his clothing and dressed quickly, pausing just long enough to read the apologetic note that said she'd been called to the station on an emergency.

Yes, he'd been sleeping deeply with her supple body in his arms, but he knew her phone hadn't made any of the obnoxious sounds she'd programmed for police business. In between rounds of lovemaking, she'd made a point of putting it on the charger next to the bed.

So, if not official business, where had she run off to so early? He didn't like the answers that immediately came to mind. Last night he'd suspected she had made a move of some sort in hopes of thwarting the enemy. Now, he was certain she was up to something she didn't want anyone else to know about. Fastening his watch, he checked the time. Two hours before the official opening of the Christmas Village.

He did a quick search on his way out. In the kitchen he found another note inviting him to help himself to coffee and whatever else he wanted and asking him to lock up as he left. Eggs and toast weren't his primary concern. He wanted her to tell him what she was up to.

He suppressed the sinking feeling in his gut as he violated her privacy and opened the laptop she'd left on the kitchen table, but it had to be done. Keeping her safely in her post as Belclare's police chief was his first order of business.

Finding the email requesting a meeting with the sleeper cell leader landed like a punch to the gut and his breath stalled in his chest. Irrational as it was, temper and a strange hurt surged through him. He knew she didn't trust him completely, and he even understood why. But to take this step without any backup was desperate. The terrorist leader would cut her down without a second thought and use her death as a cautionary tale to others who would try to prevent further operations.

He closed her computer and locked up her house, darting across the driveway to his place. He fought his first instinct to don the tactical gear and weapons stashed behind the wall in the bedroom closet—that wasn't the answer.

Instead, mustering his operational calm, he changed into jeans and a thermal shirt. He shrugged into a shoulder holster and checked the load on his 9mm. Covering the gun with a thick chamois shirt, he headed downstairs for his boots and down vest. He'd think of a reason to explain his return visit to the Christmas tree lot on the way.

Chapter Fifteen

Abby chose a spot close to the entrance of the Lewiston tree lot, not surprised her car was the only one in the parking area. She'd decided on this location because of the family and because it gave her enemy the illusion of several ways in and out.

The chicken-wire fencing didn't offer much in the way of a challenge or a deterrent to trespassers. Though they'd never suffered a threat or lost property, the Lewiston family maintained an armed watch on the lot 24/7. One of them would be around, watching.

"Welcome to your last day in my town," Abby murmured, as she checked her weapon and slid the extra clips of ammunition into her coat pockets. Provided her email had made it through to the right party and her challenge had been accepted, the terrorist grip on Belclare was about to end.

With her badge in plain view on her jacket and her Glock in hand, she stepped out of the car. The sun was bright in the sky, but the air was bitter cold. The wind nipped at her cheeks and chilled the denim of her jeans. Her boots crunched on the snow-covered gravel of the parking area. Alternately stepping and pausing to listen, her gun lowered but ready, she cautiously entered the forest of Christmas trees neatly organized by size and type.

She felt eyes on her and knew she'd drawn the attention of at least one member of the Lewiston family. Based on the increased patrols, she knew her officers could be on-site within three minutes of an emergency call. Three minutes gave her plenty of time to draw out a confession or at least identify a viable suspect.

Her radio crackled. "Mornin', Chief," a voice rasped. "One trespasser in the northeast corner. No visible weapon."

Of course the Lewistons would know the police channels. She nodded, appreciating the tip as much as the automatic cooperation. She'd just started moving with more confidence to that position when the same voice sounded off again.

"Second contact directly east of your position has a shoulder holster. Don't know what you're up to but seems like you've got some interest."

A quick prickle of fear skittered down her spine. She hadn't expected this to be easy. With a bit of clever maneuvering she could still pull this off. Failure wasn't an option.

Keeping rows of trees between her and the east side of the lot, she moved closer to the corner, eager to find who was waiting.

The sound of a shotgun rang out, sending birds into flight. The lower branches of a tree splintered on her right. Fresh pine filled the air. The tree slumped to the side and she caught sight of a familiar red vest diving for cover.

The terrorist could *not* be Riley. The words bounced around in her head. No, the jackass terrorist was messing with her. She couldn't have been so wrong as to sleep with her enemy.

"Show yourself!" She dropped to her belly, looking for boots and listening for movement. "I thought you came to negotiate."

"I believe he came to kill you."

Where was that voice coming from? And what the hell was Deke doing out here? He'd never spent so much time away from his house. Feet appeared in her line of sight but no boots. The high shine on the shoes and the dark slacks warned that it was in fact the artist who'd come to meet her. Could she have so badly misjudged the man?

She measured the distance to the man and stayed low. "What brings you out this morning, Deke?"

"I've wanted to tell you for ages, darling," he replied, not moving from his position. "I do so much more than paint."

It was him! She'd been a fool! So grateful for his help to the town's well-being—to her well-being, she hadn't seen the forest for the trees. Now, with Christmas trees surrounding her, she saw exactly what she'd been missing.

"No time like the present," Abby offered, checking Deke's position again and spotting boots moving closer to him. Tied this time, there was no mistaking Riley's footwear. If it was him, why wasn't he defending himself? And her? Her heart turned as cold as the ground beneath her chest. Tears stung her eyes. She would cry later. Right now, she had a confession to gain and an arrest to make. Maybe two.

"I'm not sure you can handle the truth, sweet Abby," Deke taunted.

Fury tightened her lips. "Your being here says it all. That email only went to my haters. That tells me a hell of a lot."

"Are you sure, Abby? More than one federal agency has been watching Belclare. I was sent to keep an eye on things…to protect you." He sounded as calm as he did over coffee in his parlor. "Do stand up and let's discuss this rationally. You know me, Abby. Why would you hide from me? If I'd wanted you dead, I could have easily made that happen on any number of occasions."

At least that last part was the truth. "Yes," she said, pushing to her feet. She'd had enough. She wanted the truth. "Why don't we all three discuss this right now."

"Agreed." Riley stepped clear of the trees he was using for cover, holding a gun aimed at Deke's chest.

Deke's gloved hands were raised and empty, palms facing out.

As if seeing him for the first time, she could tell by Riley's stance that carpentry wasn't his primary vocation. Questions ripped through her, not one of them relevant to this particular moment and all too painful. "Lower your weapon," she ordered, her voice quavering.

"No." He didn't flinch. "Deke Maynard is a killer, the mastermind behind all of this. We just got confirmation."

"The convenient lies of an expert assassin," Deke countered, shaking his head as if the accusations were nothing more serious than the ranting of an unhappy child. "I saw the media footage of him with that poor woman's car. Quite a heroic feat, designed to impress you, Abby. He's been lying to you all along. I've been doing some research of my own and Riley O'Brien is not who he claims he is."

"You know damn good and well I didn't have anything to do with any of this, Abby," Riley argued, fury darkening his face.

Deke made a disapproving *tsk-tsk.* "He got that close? You mustn't blame yourself. His specific…*ah*…skills are well-known in unsavory circles."

Abby tried to summon her voice but it wasn't happening. All she could do was watch the two men who had fooled her so completely. Maybe she didn't deserve to be Belclare's chief of police after all.

"Deke is a terrorist," Riley accused. "The dump of Filmore's phone records shows a connection."

"The man and I chatted frequently about what was best

for the town," Deke explained. "You know how obsessed he is with preservation."

Abby struggled with the decision. They were both so convincing. She searched for a defining question, one that would expose the liar. "Someone convinced Filmore to set that fire."

"A search of his home turned up nothing of consequence," Deke said, dropping his hands to his pockets with a new measure of confidence that no one was going to shoot him. "I believe he thought he could save the town by making you look bad."

Deke glanced beyond her, to her left. What was he looking for? She risked a glance in that direction, but she didn't see any movement. If someone was closing in on them, the Lewiston guard would fire or, at the very least, warn her.

"Think, Abby," Riley challenged, bringing her attention back on point. His gun was still trained on Deke.

"Lower the gun," she repeated, the mixture of hurt and anger building in her chest making it hard to breathe.

Riley shot her a disappointed look but did as she asked this time. Abby looked from Deke to Riley and back again. Her heart screamed for her to make the right choice, her temper told her to drag them both to jail.

"Yes, do think carefully," Deke said, his voice steady and smooth as silk while she wrestled with her indecision. "This man, this *stranger,* has used you to further a terrible cause."

"How long are you going to listen to this crap?" Riley demanded. "How well do you really know him, Abby?"

Deke was the eccentric artist, the local recluse who only came down from his studio to grace the people with enough wisdom and charm to keep them satisfied. And perpetually curious. Beyond weekly coffee and the occasional canvas displayed in the gallery window, what did she know about how he spent his time or where his assets came from?

She didn't want to believe he was the bad guy, but she couldn't quite believe he was a federal agent.

A wave of guilt rushed over her. She'd enjoyed his attentions, believing his interest and supportive friendship had been genuine. Had his flattery made her blind to the facts of his true nature?

"Finish this, Abby," Riley urged. "Don't make a mistake that will get us both killed."

His voice slid low and rough across her senses, much as those working hands of his had slipped over her body last night. If he was the assassin Deke claimed, Riley had certainly been close enough to take her out any number of times, as well.

It was the worst kind of standoff. She was staring at a hero and a killer. She only had to decide which one was which. Being wrong could very well cost her her life. Being right could cost her the love of her life. She nearly laughed at herself for ever thinking she enjoyed making the tough calls.

Sirens approached and brakes squealed, making the turn from the paved road into the gravel parking lot. Here was her backup—who would she send back in cuffs?

"Abby," Deke coaxed. "You know me."

"He's a liar, Abby," Riley insisted.

Her gaze locked with Riley's and suddenly she knew. Heart and gut instinct aligned in one perfect moment of clarity. Riley had warned her there was more to this situation and he'd repeatedly asked her who stood to gain. She couldn't prove it in legal terms, but she wouldn't have to. *Unless she was wrong.*

Her backup rushed into position next to her.

"Arrest Mr. Maynard," she announced. She kept her gun trained on Deke until Officer Gadsden had him handcuffed. "I'll notify Homeland Security." She risked a look at Riley. "Mr. O'Brien?"

"Yes?"

"I'll need you to come in and make a formal statement." A statement that better include a thorough explanation of that confirmation he'd mentioned, as well as his surprise appearance out here.

He arched an eyebrow. Whether that silent, subtle gesture was about her official tone or something else, she didn't care to analyze right now.

"I can do that. Anything else?"

Oh, there was a lot more, but this wasn't the place to get into the other issues. "The city of Belclare thanks you." She turned her back on him before she broke down entirely. The chief of police did not dissolve into a puddle of mush in front of terrorists and curious citizens.

"Hey, Chief!"

She looked over at Jerry Lewiston, the head of the Lewiston family. He was standing near the area Deke had been looking at. "Yes?"

"Can we keep the bomb?"

"I beg your pardon?" The shock of his words cleared away the emotional cobwebs. Thankfully.

"Way I figure, it's a fair exchange for the damaged tree."

"I'd have to disagree," she said, striding over to see what the hell he was talking about. "It's evidence."

"But it was my boy who helped your friend in the red vest disarm it and save your life."

She looked down, her knees wobbling. It had been a close call. Lewiston was right. If this had gone off... "You saw who planted it."

"I did." He lifted his chin toward Deke. "That fancy one. Probably thought we were all asleep. I guess he don't know us Lewistons too well."

The confirmation that she'd made the right choice should have been more satisfying, but all she could think about were how foolish she'd been to ever trust Deke Maynard and how many lies Riley had told her. "Just the one?"

"Yes, ma'am."

"It has to come with me."

Lewiston was clearly disappointed. She motioned him to move closer, away from the bomb. "You realize this puts me in your debt."

The man smiled, understanding. "All right then, guess that's a fair trade."

She relayed the details to the feds and assigned the appropriate instructions. When she finally settled behind the wheel of her car, she risked one more glance at Riley, who stood at the entrance watching her.

He would put Belclare behind him as soon as his statement was signed. Why wouldn't he? He had obviously been sent here.

Fine. It was for the best. Amazing sex wasn't enough reason for him to stay. Not when she couldn't trust him. Obviously, she didn't know him at all. If she were any other woman under normal circumstances, she would run straight to Riley and rest easy in the illusion of security she found in his embrace. Good grief, if she were any other woman, she wouldn't have been stuck in this impossible dilemma to start with.

If she'd been any other woman, men like Deke Maynard and Riley O'Brien might easily have overlooked her. Power, duty and responsibility were as much a part of her as her blond hair and preference for candy-apple-red toenail polish.

Apparently Deke was the only person who sensed there was any lingering naïveté to exploit. She couldn't wrap her head around how *that* revelation made her feel.

Well, she'd just have to count this a hard lesson learned. This incident marked the last time she trusted first and asked questions later—particularly when it came to men. No one else would ever be allowed close enough to hurt her.

She put the car in gear and followed the officers transporting Deke to the station.

It was over.

IN HIS TRUCK, Riley fumed every second of the short trip to the police station. "The city of Belclare thanks me, my ass."

The only thanks he wanted was a paycheck for a good day's work. He didn't want any gratitude from Belclare or the chief of police.

Well, at least the latter was partly true. What he wanted was the woman behind the badge. He needed her. More, he needed her to understand what they'd shared was real, not another facet of the game that bastard Maynard had been playing with her.

Why couldn't she tell the difference?

His hand flexed and released around the leather-wrapped steering wheel. He supposed if she couldn't tell the difference to some degree he'd be listening to one of Belclare's finest rattle off his Miranda rights about now. Her face danced across his vision. Not the lovely, poetry-quoting face of last night, but the accusing expression, full of doubt as she decided which man to believe and which to haul in.

He might be new in town, but she could hardly call him a stranger. Not after last night. Not after all that they'd shared before that. He had to find a way to make her listen. *Soul meets soul on lovers' lips.* She'd been the one to quote Shelley as her body had been draped over his like a sensual blanket last night.

She'd said those words while he'd been thinking about the ramifications of his lifelong assignment to Belclare. To her. And he'd felt the truth of her words sink deep into his system. Accepted. Known. In that moment he understood to the bone who he was: *hers*.

Nothing in his life had ever felt more perfect or so full of promise and potential than that moment. Damned if he was going to just give in and let her walk away from what they'd started. If the tables were reversed, she wouldn't let him hide.

Riley stalked into the station, his irritation with her hovering like a dark cloud over his head. He gave his statement and accepted the thank-yous for saving her life and helping to solve the mystery. It seemed he wasn't a stranger to anyone but her. He didn't need a shrink to tell him why that stung so much.

His official task complete, he lingered at the station, knowing he had to talk this out with her now rather than later. They processed the artist-terrorist, though the man showed no signs of cooperating despite Gadsden finding a remote detonator for the bomb in his pocket.

While Abby remained locked in the conference room with the mayor and some suit from Homeland Security, Riley used his phone to check email.

She had no idea how good he was at the waiting game.

Chapter Sixteen

Abby closed the door, clinging to the last thread of her control. "You've been lying to me." She pulled the cord on the blinds at the conference room window, blocking the curious gazes from her department. "About everything."

"Not everything," Riley countered.

"The only reason you aren't in cuffs is because you saved Mrs. Wilks."

"And you."

Her breath stuttered at his audacity. She hated that he was right. That she'd been duped. "And me," she agreed through clenched teeth. "Though I would have managed without you. My plan to draw out the terrorist worked."

"Apparently, but you were up against—"

"What? Who?" She was shouting. Clamping her lips together, she stopped until she could regain control. "Sit down and tell me everything you think you know about the threats against me." As he took a seat, she settled into her chair and carefully removed her .40 caliber Glock, placing it on the table. "Convince me you aren't one of those threats."

He glanced at the weapon before meeting her gaze. "I think you know better."

She didn't. Not now. She wanted to believe him, desperately, but that was thinking with her heart. Here, under these circumstances, being a cop trumped being a woman.

Homeland Security had briefed her about a new task force that placed agents in suspect, high-risk areas.

Apparently Riley was a one-man task force. And though that didn't make him the enemy, it made him the man who'd lied to her…used her. "You said you had confirmation of Deke's involvement." The feds had denied that claim. They were executing a search of his house now.

When this was resolved, when she knew what he was really doing in her town, then she could berate herself for sleeping with him, for falling for the lies—spoken and unspoken.

"Abby," he began.

"Chief Jensen," she corrected.

"Chief Jensen," he echoed, tension in his tone. "You really don't have the cl—"

"If you finish that sentence with 'clearance' I will shoot you on principle."

"A stunt like that means a lot of paperwork."

"Accidents happen. Firearms are dangerous."

SO ARE YOU, Riley thought, deciding maybe he shouldn't twitch a muscle. "So put it away," he suggested. He didn't think the weapon was nearly as deadly as the woman on the other side of the table. "Where are you holding Mr. Maynard?"

"That isn't your concern."

He should have told her last night, security clearances be damned. He'd wanted to tell her she wasn't in this alone the night one of Maynard's lackeys had pushed Calder off the ladder.

Now it was too late. Her gorgeous blue gaze had turned icy. She felt betrayed and he could hardly blame her. Ironic really, that when he knew just who he wanted to be and why, when his identity felt more real and true than any other time in his life, the woman he wanted to be real for wouldn't believe in him.

"Mr. O'Brien?"

"Riley," he said, frustrated by her insistence on reverting to these formalities. He couldn't leave town even if he wanted to. Director Casey had planted him here for a reason. Belclare was still a ripe target. Whatever she believed, this wasn't over yet.

"Start talking or I'm dumping you in a holding cell."

"On what charge?" He jerked a thumb over his shoulder. "All of Belclare thinks I'm a hero."

"I suppose that was your plan. Waltz into my town, win over the locals and seduce the little-lady police chief."

No one thought of her that way. "Last night was no one-sided seduction," he said, leaning forward, ignoring the damned gun on the desk.

"Let's stick with today," she snapped, color flooding her cheeks. "Who are you? Start with your real name."

He gripped the arms of the chair. Might as well spill it all—he doubted she would grant him another chance to clear the air. "I have no idea what my real name is. Riley O'Brien is what the teachers and staff in the orphanage called me. When I graduated, I traded a few years in the military for college tuition. Now I'm here."

"No Irish parents?"

"Your guess is as good as mine." He shook his head. His childhood fantasies of home and hearth felt silly now. The fragile new hope she'd kindled sputtered out beneath her unrelenting blue gaze.

"There seems to be a significant gap in your personal history."

"I agree." He refused to elaborate, even if it was possible. Whether or not she hated him for what they shared on a personal level, Belclare was his post and he wouldn't jeopardize that. If he was exposed or ousted, who would protect her?

Let her hate him for lying about his past, but she'd come to mean too much in such a short time for him to walk away and leave her safety to someone else.

"Who sent you here?" Her eyes flared as something else occurred to her. "What in the hell did you do to the Hamiltons?"

He rolled his eyes, aggravated by her suddenly over-active imagination. "Call the Realtor, check in on them. I showed you the paperwork. You know I came by the house honestly when I was decorating the realty office storefront."

She scoffed at that, her fingertips dancing along the grip of her gun.

This really couldn't get any worse. Unless she shot him. "Call. Verify my story. I'm not going anywhere."

"Oh, yes, you are. Tell me the truth and then get out of my town."

"I told you the truth." At least as much as he dared to explain right now. Deke was in custody, but were the men who did his dirty work planning to follow through on what-ever orders he'd already issued? It was too soon to tell. If he could get Abby to calm down, he had a feeling she'd agree with his assessment.

He was furious that Deke had managed to expose him and kill her trust. From Riley's vantage point, exposing him gave anyone a clear shot at Abby.

"The *whole* truth."

The only truth that mattered to Riley was sitting on the other side of the desk. Abby had started as an assignment, but she was so much more now. He didn't think she wanted to hear that. She wouldn't want to hear how he admired this side of her. Even with her substantial fury leveled at him, he admired her. Wanted her. He shook his head. "The truth that matters is I am here to protect you and your town from a very real terrorist threat. Your success this morning notwithstanding, my orders have not changed. You don't have the authority to send me anywhere." Not professionally anyway, but he left that unsaid.

She swore, impressing him with her colorful vocabulary. "The explosives are secure. The man using the docks and this town as his personal criminal playground is in custody. Belclare is safe again. You can go."

But the threat against her personally, the promise to make her an example, still loomed over her head. "I have to stay." He pushed to his feet. "I'm sorry that makes you uncomfortable, Abby."

His heart clutched when she picked up her gun, but she returned it carefully to her purse as she pushed to her feet, as well.

"Mr. O'Brien, I don't want to see you. Not next door, not in my station, not at the pub. Stick to your so-called orders if you must, but stay out of my sight."

"On one condition."

"You don't get to name conditions here!" She trembled with the fury she obviously felt.

He wasn't leaving until he'd warned her. "Keep someone with you. I don't think this is over."

"Is that a threat?"

"Of course not," he said. It felt like one of those shipping containers was sitting on his chest. This might be the last time he was this close to her—he couldn't let fear ruin it.

"I'll stay out of your sight, but I'm next door if you ever need me."

"I won't."

He believed her. He paused with one hand on the door-knob and turned back to face her. "Last night—"

"Don't you dare say it."

"—was everything to me," he finished.

"Get out." Her hands fisted at her sides and he knew she wanted to throw something.

"You asked for the truth." He left the room and walked out of the station, wishing the back door was still an option. He kept his gaze straight ahead, avoiding eye contact with everyone.

When Danny called out, Riley just raised a hand, unwilling to pause for a conversation. Tomorrow would be a better day. The sting of embarrassment would ease and she'd calm down. She might never forgive him, but out of sight or not, he was determined to keep her safe enough to enjoy a long life of hating him.

He was backing out of his parking space when his cell phone rang. The caller ID showed a blocked number and Riley flinched as he pulled back into the parking space to take the call.

"That takedown looks good," Director Casey said in his ear.

"News travels fast."

"You don't sound happy. Is there more?"

"I think so. She arrested Deke Maynard, but it was too easy," Riley said, finally able to articulate what bothered him most. "The bomb he'd planted was elementary. Anyone could have disarmed it."

"You expected someone with more tactical experience?"

"If a threat is serious enough to incite this much concern across federal agencies, then yes, I expect to encounter experienced people on the ground, too."

"Sleeper cells are often populated with civilians. It's the definition."

"Soft is one thing. Ignorant is another. You can't pull me out yet."

"I wasn't planning to. Long-term and indefinite, remember?"

Riley took a deep, relieved breath. "Thanks."

"Got a theory?"

"Deke Maynard has his eye on Chief Jensen. He might be a master strategist with all the crap he's managed here, but I think somewhere along the line it became personal."

"Artists can be twitchy."

"Sure," Riley admitted, though he had little experience. "They're searching his place and squeezing the butler for info."

"The analysts will sort it out."

"Thank you."

"One more thing," Casey said. "A new version of her speech on YouTube surfaced an hour ago. We've blocked it and we're tracing the party who loaded it."

"How was it modified?"

"Red crosshairs over her face and different scenery. The analysts haven't sorted out the background yet, but the landscape is covered with snow. We can't tell if the images are current or older. So it appears your hunch is correct. Stay close to her."

"No problem," Riley lied. "Can you send it to me?"

"Already done."

"Thank you, sir."

"If you need backup, just say the word. We can get someone into place now, before any more trouble hits."

"Yes, sir. I'll let you know."

The kind of backup he really needed, Director Casey couldn't provide. No amount of tactical expertise would fix the mess he'd made here.

He pulled up the video on his phone and his blood ran

cold. The new images in the background ranged from the current display in the park to the podium in front of the scorched police station where Abby had given her latest press conference.

But it was the angle of the photos that told Riley all he needed to know. He sent the request for backup, knowing the assassin was about to make his move. Regardless of how Abby felt about him personally, he would implement protective measures. No detail was too small, no request too big if it meant keeping her alive.

Chapter Seventeen

For the first time since the fire, Abby was grateful her office had been charred. She wasn't even upset the cleanup was taking longer than promised. Working at home would be for the best. Despite the proximity to Riley, at home behind closed doors and drawn curtains she could cry. Scream into a pillow. Her mascara could streak down her face and her nose could turn Rudolph-red. At home, no one could watch her fall apart.

She couldn't believe Maynard had gotten bail. Evidently he owned at least one judge—a man Abby thought she knew. Of course, Maynard had been forced to surrender his passport. So what? The man could have twenty for all anyone knew.

This day could not suck any worse.

She pulled all the way into her garage this time, unwilling to risk even a glimpse of Riley. Hurrying to the house, she dropped her purse on the table and drew the curtains in her kitchen and den.

But nothing blotted out the scent of her Christmas tree. A day ago it had been the best scent ever. Now, she felt nauseous. Reluctantly, she walked down the hallway. Like ripping off a bandage, she had to get this over with and find a way to rid him from her system. Her knees quivering, she turned into the front room.

And stalled.

"Welcome home, my dear." Deke, standing in the middle of the room, revealed a gun, raising it until the barrel was even with her chest.

Abby saw the cold death in his eyes, knew making a run was futile. How could she have been so wrong about him? "You'll never get away with this."

"Darling, I already have. Reliable witnesses are ready to testify they saw me at my attorney's office during the time of your tragic death."

His hand was too steady. She was out of time and options. Her gun was in her purse where she'd left it in the kitchen.

She sidestepped around the coffee table.

Deke wagged a finger. "No, no. Just take a seat. This will all be over shortly."

"What?" She stayed on her feet. "You're going to make this look like a suicide?" She had to keep him talking. "People know me better than that." She had to think of something.

He tipped his head to the side. "It was a thought. But you're right. And the damage lasts longer if your killer might be roaming free in Belclare."

"You're a monster. You worked Filmore into a frenzy."

"No," he snapped, stepping forward. "Filmore was his own worst enemy. The man was a small cog in a large machine. I am much more valuable. You might have been an asset, but instead you became an impediment. Now you must go. And don't worry, my attorneys will prove your pathetic police work was all wrong. You can die knowing you didn't stop me."

He was insane. Unfortunately, he'd focused all of that insanity on her. There was no babbling remorse over what he'd done or what he was about to do. His confidence unnerved her, but she refused to give in without a fight.

He'd moved drugs through her town, nearly killed two of her neighbors, three if she counted Riley, and burned down her police station. No, she would not give in while she still had an ounce of breath in her lungs.

"Why don't you just go?" she whispered. She needed him to believe she was completely beaten. "I'll let you walk away. I'll tell the world I was wrong." She forced herself to sit on the edge of the couch and reached out to trace the soft petal of a rose in the flowers he'd brought her yesterday.

Deke laughed, the sound harsh and laced with violent intent. "Oh, you might give me a head start, but you'd never give up or lie. You have far too much integrity. I sincerely regret to say that is your downfall."

"You'd be the white whale, too big for me to ever catch."

"How you tempt me." He came around the coffee table and sat beside her with that elegant grace she used to admire and now detested. "Unfortunately for you, I am a greedy white whale and the bounty on your head has become more than I can resist. You see, bigger fish than I want you gone."

He reached out, taking a lock of her hair and winding it around his fingers. "I did have hopes for you. For us."

"Tell me," she whispered, trying to hide how he made her skin crawl. She had to disarm him, it was her only hope.

There was a creak on the stairs and everything in him shifted. His eyes darted in that direction and then back to her, his features twisting into an evil snarl. His hand fisted in her hair and he yanked her head back. The muzzle of the gun was cold against the tender skin under her jaw. "Come out or I'll blow off her head!" he shouted.

Abby went still, fighting the instinct to squirm. "Who are you talking to?"

"Your lover, I'm sure. I cannot believe you took up with him. You don't even know him. He's lied to you every bit as much as I have!"

She hated that Deke was right, but then again, she'd known Deke for years and had never seen this darkness in him.

Maybe she was a fool.

"No one is here, Deke," she said. Everyone thought the bad guy was caught. She'd pushed Riley away after learning the truth. If she didn't think of some way out of this, she'd never have the chance to apologize. Intense regret swamped her. She squeezed her eyes shut against a sudden rush of tears, but one escaped, trickling back into her hair.

"Who are you crying for, darling?"

The endearment, so ugly in Deke's elitist tones, snapped her out of her self-pity.

"Kill me or run," she said, gathering her courage. "But make a damned decision already." She elbowed him in the gut and stomped on his foot. It wasn't an effective strike at this angle, but it forced the gun from her face and the distraction bought her precious seconds. He still had her by the hair. She pulled her knees to her chest and kicked out, hitting him in the chest and forcing the air from his lungs.

His fingers released her. A wild shot exploded from the weapon and breezed by her head. He shouted more threats as she rolled to the floor, but she ignored them all, searching for any kind of weapon. Her coffee table splintered and the vase toppled, spilling water all over her.

Deke swore, lunging for her again. She grabbed the vase and bashed him over the head.

Another gunshot rang out, and Deke's body went limp, crushing hers.

The coppery smell of fresh blood mixed with the clean

pine and sweet roses and lilies that had brightened the room so cheerfully just a day ago.

She pushed at Deke's shoulders, not sure if he was dead or merely unconscious. The floor shook as people pounded into her house.

Then she was surrounded by people dressed in black tactical SWAT gear. She only knew they weren't from Belclare, or even Baltimore. The team lifted Deke's body off her, carrying him and his gun out of her house. She asked if he was dead, but no one answered her.

"Are you injured?"

She shook her head. Only her coffee table and a wall or two. The raw wounds she suffered wouldn't benefit from a bandage.

"Someone will contact you for a statement," one of the team said, and then he walked away.

The sudden quiet in their absence was nearly as shocking as their entrance had been.

She pushed up to the couch, but it felt slimy. Contaminated by Deke's deception and violence. Raking her hair back from her face, her knees wobbled as she tried to walk away from the destroyed room. She just couldn't face the mess and destruction right now. Couldn't cope with all that it signified.

The bathroom upstairs was too far. She might as well climb Mount Everest. She stepped out of her shoes and stumbled along to the kitchen.

A man clad in black tactical gear filled the room, his back to her. He didn't have a helmet and she recognized the sandy-brown hair as well as the spread of his shoulders. Shoulders she'd leaned on more than once in past days. Shoulders she'd clung to last night with part of him deep inside her. "Riley?"

Her hand covered her lips. Was that even his name?

"Have a seat, Abby."

"You…" She looked back toward the hallway. "You're here to take my statement?"

"Eventually. Right now I just want to take care of you."

"I'm fine."

He stripped off his bulletproof vest and set it on the floor by the back door. "You're in shock."

"On a few levels," she confessed. "You saved my life." He'd said that was his job, his real purpose in Belclare.

"I had a little help."

"But I said…" She had to clear away the emotion clogging her throat. "I said awful things at the station."

"I might have deserved them." He shrugged. "I hurt you." He ran warm water over a paper towel, then squeezed out the excess. Pulling another chair closer, he started cleaning her face.

"I can do that," she protested, abruptly annoyed by his tenderness. He should be angry with her. She should still be angry with him. What did it mean that he was here? Was he just doing his job again or was there more to it?

It scared her how much she wanted there to be more to it.

He washed her face and sat back, staring at her. There were questions in his soft brown gaze that echoed the ones chasing through her mind.

"You handled yourself well," he said.

"Is he dead?"

"Don't know," Riley answered. "Does it matter?"

"Only if he causes more trouble."

"Well, dead or alive, I can assure you Deke Maynard is done causing trouble."

"You're sure about that?"

He nodded. "No lawyer will get him off or out on bail now."

She believed him. She should ask for proof, but it was

there in his steady, golden-brown gaze. He was telling her the truth.

"I want a new couch," she blurted.

"That's reasonable."

"This time I want it bigger."

One of his dark eyebrows arched and his lips twitched at the corner. "Big enough for two?"

She nodded. "Maybe a sectional."

He laughed and pulled her to her feet, wrapping his arms around her. "Now we have two houses needing repair work."

Abby spread her hands flat across his chest, stroking up and over his shoulders, following the firm muscles under the black ribbed sweater down to his hands. "I know a guy who's good with his hands." She lifted his hands to her lips, kissing each finger in turn.

"You do?"

She looked up into his warm brown eyes and felt the weight of the world simply fall away. "I do."

"Took you long enough to decide between us today."

She wondered if he could forgive her hesitation or if it would be the end of them after all. "I was wrong but there were mitigating circumstances."

"Let's talk about those circumstances."

"You know," she said, trying not to look at him, "you're free to go now. You got the bad guy. Saved my life—again."

"I wish that was true."

"What does that mean?" Did she even want to know?

She slumped against him, too tired for games. Riley had proved himself a jack-of-all-trades, from hanging garland to making her feel treasured *in* bed as well as out of it. Here, behind closed doors, no one was watching; she could lean in and steal a kiss and no one could call her weak. No one could judge her momentary lapse from police chief to normal woman.

Before temptation got the better of her, Riley came to her rescue again. He gently cradled her face in his palms, holding her steady for his kiss. She watched him close the distance, her eyes drifting shut as his lips met hers. But the kiss was fleeting, not deep as she'd hoped and his breath whispered across her face.

"I'm not free."

She opened her eyes, caught in the tender, golden-brown gaze assessing her. "What?"

"You have me well and truly caught, Abby Jensen."

She was so confused, so worried he might have to go— or want to go. "What do you want from me?"

"What I've never had." He smoothed a hand over her hair, his eyes searching hers. "I want roots. A home and family. *You,* forever."

It was mutual. *It was so mutual.* How did he pack so much intensity and intention into those few words? Her heart stuttered. She'd never really understood that a stuttering heart was possible until now. Forever was monumental. Wasn't it? She barely knew him. But forever was plenty of time to get to know him. There she went, arguing with herself!

"Think about it," he said, the words soft and warm against her lips. "I'm not leaving Belclare. I'm here to stay."

"Why?" She wanted him to kiss her the way he had last night when the world and all its problems had simply vanished. She wanted a kiss that blanked her mind and didn't leave room for questions about the past or present. A kiss that didn't carry any worries for the future.

"You know why," he murmured as his lips landed warm and soft on hers.

What started gently escalated as she wound her arms

around his waist, drawing him closer and pouring her heart into it. She wanted him to feel what she was too afraid to say. Too afraid to ask. How strange when her heart felt so safe that the rest of her trembled with fear.

Her career, her life's work, meant facing fear potentially every day. But here, with Riley, she knew there was more at stake and none of it was within her control.

Well, not much of it anyway.

He broke the kiss and studied her face. "You're thinking."

She couldn't deny it. "About you. Me. Us."

"*Us* works."

"Yes, I think it does." She took a deep breath and blurted out what neither of them could afford to overlook. "Homeland made it clear I'm still a target."

Riley rolled his eyes, but he didn't step away. "Tell me Mayor Scott didn't hear them."

"He did," she said with a smile, "but this is about you. I can handle the mayor."

"I'm not leaving." He drew her body up tight against his. "Not leaving town." He kissed her nose. "Not leaving you." He kissed her lips. "Not leaving us."

"Because of your assignment?" She hated the way her voice wobbled on the question.

"Because of *you*. I love you. Get used to it."

She pushed up on her toes and kissed him again. "I can do that."

"And?"

"And what?" she teased, trailing a fingertip along his full lower lip. He caught her finger in his teeth and growled just a little. "Oh. I have to say it?"

Another low rumble sounded in his throat.

"But I thought you knew."

He bit down a smidge harder and she laughed. "All right.

I love you, too." She tugged her finger away. "Whether you're a carpenter or a bodyguard or just the hunk next door, I love you, too. *Forever.*"

Epilogue

Thomas Casey read the report from Specialist O'Brien, pleased with the reduced threat rating for Belclare. Chief Jensen wasn't exactly in the clear—she might never be— but at least she had the best possible protection in place.

Thomas stared at the mountain of folders on his desk. Belclare was only the beginning.

* * * * *

REQUEST YOUR FREE BOOKS!
2 FREE NOVELS PLUS 2 FREE GIFTS!

HARLEQUIN

INTRIGUE

BREATHTAKING ROMANTIC SUSPENSE

YES! Please send me 2 FREE Harlequin Intrigue® novels and my 2 FREE gifts (gifts are worth about $10). After receiving them, if I don't wish to receive any more books, I can return the shipping statement marked "cancel." If I don't cancel, I will receive 6 brand-new novels every month and be billed just $4.74 per book in the U.S. or $5.24 per book in Canada. That's a savings of at least 14% off the cover price! It's quite a bargain! Shipping and handling is just 50¢ per book in the U.S. and 75¢ per book in Canada.* I understand that accepting the 2 free books and gifts places me under no obligation to buy anything. I can always return a shipment and cancel at any time. Even if I never buy another book, the two free books and gifts are mine to keep forever.

182/382 HDN F42N

Name	(PLEASE PRINT)

Address	Apt. #

City	State/Prov.	Zip/Postal Code

Signature (If under 18, a parent or guardian must sign)

Mail to the Harlequin® Reader Service:
IN U.S.A.: P.O. Box 1867, Buffalo, NY 14240-1867
IN CANADA: P.O. Box 609, Fort Erie, Ontario L2A 5X3

**Are you a subscriber to Harlequin Intrigue books
and want to receive the larger-print edition?
Call 1-800-873-8635 or visit www.ReaderService.com.**

* Terms and prices subject to change without notice. Prices do not include applicable taxes. Sales tax applicable in N.Y. Canadian residents will be charged applicable taxes. Offer not valid in Quebec. This offer is limited to one order per household. Not valid for current subscribers to Harlequin Intrigue books. All orders subject to credit approval. Credit or debit balances in a customer's account(s) may be offset by any other outstanding balance owed by or to the customer. Please allow 4 to 6 weeks for delivery. Offer available while quantities last.

Your Privacy—The Harlequin® Reader Service is committed to protecting your privacy. Our Privacy Policy is available online at www.ReaderService.com or upon request from the Harlequin Reader Service.

We make a portion of our mailing list available to reputable third parties that offer products we believe may interest you. If you prefer that we not exchange your name with third parties, or if you wish to clarify or modify your communication preferences, please visit us at www.ReaderService.com/consumerschoice or write to us at Harlequin Reader Service Preference Service, P.O. Box 9062, Buffalo, NY 14269. Include your complete name and address.

HI13R

SPECIAL EXCERPT FROM

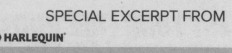

HARLEQUIN®

INTRIGUE®

Read on for a sneak peek of
DELIVERANCE AT CARDWELL RANCH
by New York Times *bestselling author*

B.J. Daniels

Part of the **CARDWELL COUSINS** *series*

**Daniels delivers another Cardwell Ranch keeper
with a woman on the run…and the lawman sworn
to keep her safe.**

"Maybe you don't understand the fine line between
snooping and jail. Breaking and entering is—"

"I'm going with you." Donning a hat and gloves,
Gillian turned to look at him.

Austin was smiling at her as if amused.

"What?" she said, suddenly feeling uncomfortable
under his scrutiny. She knew it was silly. He'd seen her at
her absolute worst.

"You just look so…cute," he said. "Clearly, breaking
the law excites you."

She smiled in spite of herself. It had been a while since
a man had complimented her. But it wasn't breaking the
law that excited her.

She breathed in the freezing air. It stung her lungs,
but made her feel more alive than she had in years. Fear
drove her steps along with hope.

At the dark alley, Austin slowed. It was late enough
that there were lights on in the houses.

HIEXP69800

"Come on," Austin said, and they started to turn down the alley.

A vehicle came around the corner, moving slowly. Gillian felt the headlights wash over them, and she let out a worried sound as she froze in midstep.

Her moment of panic didn't subside when she saw that it was a sheriff's department vehicle.

"Austin?" she whispered, not sure what to do.

He turned to her and pulled her into his arms. Her mouth opened in surprise, and the next thing she knew, he was kissing her. At first, she was too stunned to react. But after a moment, she put her arms around his neck and lost herself in the kiss.

As the headlights of the sheriff's car washed over them, she let out a small helpless moan as Austin deepened the kiss, drawing her even closer.

The sheriff's car went on past, and she felt a pang of regret. Slowly, Austin drew back a little. His gaze locked with hers, and for a moment they stood like that, their quickened warm breaths coming out in white clouds.

"Sorry."

She shook her head. She wasn't sorry. She felt...light-headed, happy, as if helium-filled. She thought she might drift off into the night if he let go of her.

"Are you okay?" he asked, looking worried.

She touched the tip of her tongue to her lower lip. "Great. Never better."

Find out what happens next in
DELIVERANCE AT CARDWELL RANCH
by New York Times *bestselling author B.J. Daniels,*
available December 2014,
only from Harlequin Intrigue.